YOU GOTTA DANCE

Inspired by a true story

YOU GOTTA DANCE

Inspired by a true story

by

Michael Daluz and Bryant K. Daluz

iUniverse, Inc.
New York Bloomington

You Gotta Dance

iUniverse books may be ordered through booksellers or by contacting:

iUniverse
1663 Liberty Drive
Bloomington, IN 47403
www.iuniverse.com
1-800-Authors (1-800-288-4677)

ISBN: 978-1-4401-4169-0 (pbk)
ISBN: 978-1-4401-4167-6 (dj)
ISBN: 978-1-4401-4168-3 (ebk)

Printed in the United States of America

iUniverse rev. date: 5/5/2009

"You Gotta Dance"

Synopsis by
Bryant K. Daluz

"You Gotta Dance" is based on the life of a man from Connecticut who endures crushing trials that put him on the path to a remarkable spiritual recovery, and eventual success. In 1987, Michael Daluz, a black U.S. Army veteran and college student, is beaten nearly to death by a mob of white males as he and two buddies leave a local off-campus bar. He fires a single shot from his handgun, critically injuring one of the attackers. This act of self-defense leads to his arrest and imprisonment. Before sentencing, Michael succumbs to drug use, criminal activity and a bitter hatred.

During his incarceration, he experiences an inner transformation, which prepares him for another personal tragedy: a near-fatal, work-related accident that leaves him severely injured. Putting his faith in God, he decides to challenge his multi-million-dollar employer in a civil lawsuit. At the same time, he has to fight for custody of his young daughter, pursue his medical education and continue to inspire other people to change.

"MICHAEL'S ACKNOWLEDGEMENTS"

Michael Daluz (To Give Light). Thank you, God, for changing my life and allowing me to inspire other people by sharing how great you are. Thank you, Yvonne, Edward and Teba Henderson and my entire family for their support. A special acknowledgement goes to my daughters, Bella, Heaven and Morgan Daluz. Each of you has a special place in my heart. I love you. I would like to thank the U.S. Army for teaching me pride and honor. Thank you, Dr. Brett Rayford, Derik Harrison and Antonio Coles for believing in me and giving me the chance to become successful. Thank you, Dwayne McBride, Latannia Carey, Kirk Gordon, Jack Deluce, the original Miami Nightbreederz family, and my F-Troop family. Always remember my motto, "Why be good, when you can be great and never stop dancing"!

"BRYANT'S ACKNOWLEDGEMENTS"

First and foremost, I would like to thank Michael for giving me the opportunity to write and for trusting me with his story. I would also like to thank my mom and dad for always standing by me, and instilling me with an abundance of love. Mom, you did a wonderful job thank you for the strong spiritual foundation. To my grandmothers, Lillian Daluz and Eleanor Caldwell, I love you. To momma, thanks for all the adventures and wisdom. To my big brother, Terryl, you are the reason I do what I do today, you're the best! To my brothers, Patrick "Pity" Manick and Shonne Gibson, thanks for the years of inspiration, you guys are geniuses. My nephews Jabari and Elijah, I love you. To Ms. Renee Foreman, thanks for everything, much love to you, I wish you much success in any and everything you do. And to the rest of my family, I love you.

- 1 -

The bible says that God reveals himself to every man in his due time. Although I believed in God and prayed to him, I had no personal relationship with God.

My name is Michael Daluz and this is my spiritual journey to peace. It has led me to a better understanding of God and the purpose he has given my life. The turning point for me came one Friday night in August 2002. It was a sultry 98 degrees, on the money. I loved Fridays. Not because it was the end of the work week, but at one point in my journey I used to pick up my little girl, Bella, for the weekend from my ex-wife Tracey. Let me first tell you about Tracey.

Tracey was Panamanian, five feet three inches tall, with long jet-black hair flowing down the middle of her back. What first caught my eye about her was her alluring, buttery skin. Man, was she beautiful! She could stop traffic. None of that mattered, because I soon found out she was screwed up in the head. No fault of her own. She never knew her father and her mother died in a car accident when she was only nine years old. She went from one foster home to another, where she was abused—which may explain her "trust issues."

The way Tracey and I met was straight out of a Hollywood movie. I was a club promoter and an owner of an independent record company here in Miami. She was a model. One night, I get invited to a video shoot for a chart-topping R&B band. Here I am in the middle of a hot conversation with two of the sexiest females I've ever laid eyes on, when Tracey comes in. She's wearing high heels, and a tight-fitting black dress that falls on her like a glove. She completely steals the show. It's as if time had come to a halt. Every guy in the joint has his tongue out, and they all surround her like a pack of ravenous wolves. They point and gawk, but they don't know what to say.

I keep cool before making my move.

Once the dunce-cap guys back off, I excuse myself from the ladies, with whom I've planned to conduct my own video shoot later that night, and introduce myself to Tracey.

"Hello. I'm Michael," I confidently say.

"Hi, Michael. I'm Tracey," she answers in a tone of voice I judged engaging.

I extend my hand. "It's a pleasure to meet you, Tracey." She accepts my hand, but her skin is so soft I just about melt into her. I can only imagine what it would be like to make love to her.

"Today is the happiest day of my life, and do you know why?" I say.

"Why?" Tracey asks with a smirk.

"Because I met my wife and the mother of my children," I say, thinking I've caught her off-guard with this remark or she'll take it for a cheesy line and walk away.

We keep chatting for about 45 minutes or so, after which we decide to ditch the joint for a more romantic setting. We go for a ride in my brand new '99 BMW convertible along Ocean Drive, South Beach. We converse until sunrise. It's as though I have known this woman my entire life.

That was how we began.

After that night we saw each other regularly and got married six months later, in late 1999. That was the year I relocated to Miami. My hometown had been the small inner city of New Haven, Connecticut. It was home to the popular Yale University and a real nightmare to me. Everybody knew everybody else's business. It was like a bad soap opera, and Miami was my escape.

But as the old saying goes, *You can run but you can't hide.*

When I got to Miami, I was visited with a new set of troubles, and my marriage to Tracey lasted no more than two and a half years. In the beginning, everything between went perfect; every moment was like our honeymoon. I'm talking mind-blowing lovemaking four to five times a day, candlelit dinners and bubble baths. Tracey loved to bathe me from head to toe and feed me fresh fruit. With all I was going through at the time, I was glad to have her by my side: my first failed marriage, not being allowed to see my eldest daughter (whom I had out of wedlock), numerous back surgeries and the up-and-down rollercoaster ride of the music business.

Then, overnight and without warning, Tracey turned into a different person. She became erratic and emotional. She seemed unable to make simple decisions, turning trivial situations into major issues. She spent days, sometimes weeks, demanding not to be touched. At one point, she started to act violently towards me and herself. But then she turned around and began to project her own impulses onto me among her friends and family, claiming I was being unfaithful and abusing her. Now, I'm a fighter, but I *do not* hit women! The fact was that I loved her more than I loved myself. My guess was that the pressures of being a wife combined with her rocky childhood began to unravel her. She had no idea what it would be like to be a housewife. Her only familiarity before marriage was with glamour, or rather her craving for it—she yearned to be a trophy girlfriend on the arm of any rich cat who happened to be climbing the ladder of success.

The upshot was that our relationship spiraled out of control and I couldn't take it anymore. I filed for divorce after Thanksgiving Day, 2001.

So, we're going through the separation and she tells me that she's three months pregnant. I had no idea; she didn't show at all. Then, she informs me of her plan to get an abortion. I beg her not to, but my pleas fall on deaf ears. Needless to say, this ended up firing up the animus between us tenfold. So, I let her know that if she had the baby and didn't want to be bothered, I would take full custody of it. Finally, she buckled and gave birth to beautiful Bella, in April 02.

I called my daughter Bella Bear, she was so precious to me! She looked just like her mom, and in the months following our split, I couldn't help seeing Tracey in my daughter's face. But we harbored so much ill feeling toward one another that I recognized the beauty only in Bella's face. Looking at Bella filled me with love and a sense of purpose. She made me forget the material things I had lost in the split—a Miami Lakes apartment located in a small gated community, the BWM convertible, etc. Completely broke, I purchased a rusty '91 Toyota Celica from a friend who owned a garage. I didn't care. All that mattered was that I got to see my daughter.

Anyway, here I am pulling up to Tracey's apartment to pick up my daughter, that hot Friday night, August 2002. I climb out of my car and walk up to the front steps of her building. I hear Bella screaming uncontrollably at the top of her lungs. I look up at her room window and discover Tracey pacing back and forth yelling at her and squeezing her stuffed animal. "*Shut up! Stop crying!*" I hear her yelling.

I ring the doorbell, expecting Tracey to open up, but she doesn't. I holler at the window, "Tracey, buzz me in!"

She pokes her head out the window wearing the wickedest look on her face. She seems almost possessed. "What do you want?" she asks fiercely.

"Don't play with me, just bring Bella downstairs. And why is she crying like that?"

"Your daughter's crazy—that's why she's crying. I've been listening to this screaming for hours," she yells, then turns her head back inside to shout some more at my little girl. "If she doesn't stop this noise, I'm going to hurt her!"

"You better not touch my daughter! Now open the door," I insist, but she just sneers at me, before bursting into a giggle so eerie and grotesque I think only an insane person could sound like this.

"You know what, Michael? Carlos and I have decided that you won't be seeing Bella anymore," she announces.

Carlos, Tracey's new boyfriend, had just signed with the Pittsburgh Steelers. I'm not mentioning this out of envy. You see, I'd done it all. I had lived the champagne-popping lifestyle, the clubs, a nice house, expensive cars. Seeing my luck down, though, Tracey had already gone back on the prowl for her next moneymaker—her MO. I really didn't care about her or her love life. I just wanted the madness to end and to raise my daughter properly. That dude may be running Tracey's life but he had no say when it came to my baby girl. But God must have seen how I'd lost focus of what he had been trying to show me and wanted to get me back on the straight and narrow path.

Standing there outside Tracey's building alerts me to the fact that it's this kind of hysteria that has sent me packing in the first place. After our screaming match, she swings Bella's stuffed bear at me and slams the window shut. The bear is ripped in half. She then starts throwing things about in Bella's room, and that's when I say to myself, *Oh, hell no, I'm getting my baby!*

Despite all that'd been going on between Tracey and me, I didn't think she'd ever harm our daughter. A few times, though, when I had Bella over and was bathing her, I noticed small bruises on her body. I would confront Tracey about it. But she'd just shrug and say, "Oh, she fell."

Standing outside the door, I try my best to ward off her spite, just as I've had to do so many times before. Finally, I succumb to the darker side of me. I ram the front door with my shoulder a few times, until it caves in. The building has three floors, eight apartments each, shiny marble floors, and an old-fashioned elevator from the 1940s with one of those heavy doors that you have to be the strongest man alive to open or close.

I run like a lightning bolt up three flights of stairs, growing angrier with each step. The climb doesn't wind me. I am a U.S. army veteran and used to play little-league baseball as a kid for the New Haven Knights. My high-school dream back then was to play professional baseball. I probably could have, too. Instead I enrolled in the armed forced to serve my country. So, I am just as dedicated to protecting my little girl now as I was my country's security. At the top of the staircase, I hear Bella bawling frantically and Tracey out of her mind in rage. "I shoulda gotten ridda you when I had the chance," she screams at her daughter.

Sweating heavily, I scurry down the short, empty corridor, which is dimly illuminated by two flickering lights. My heart is in my throat at the thought of any harm coming to Bella. I pound on the door. "Tracey, open up!"

"Get away from my door, Michael!"

I kick at the door in frustration. "Tracey, I'm not gonna let you hurt my daughter!"

"Get out of here or I'll call the police!"

I step back a little then slam my body hard on the door. Next thing I know I'm standing right smack in the middle of her small living room, with its jungle-like decorations, three fern trees, the large aquarium of exotic fish I purchased back in the days when I had money, hardwood floor, black leather sofa, loveseat kitty-corning each side of the room, and of course the big-screen television against the left side of the wall.

After a few anxious glances, I race through the living room crying out, "Bella, Bella Bear. Don't worry, baby girl, Daddy got you," hoping to comfort my little girl.

I head straight for her room. But then Tracey explodes out of the kitchen with a butcher knife in her hand. Fortunately, I catch her movement from the corner of my eye and dodge the sharp blade in the nick of time. She keeps swinging at me maniacally, so I yank her by the hair and throw her to the ground. She hits her head hard on the floor and instantly blacks out.

I walk into the bedroom where Bella is lying in her crib, her muscles tense and tears raining down her usually rosy cheeks, which are now beet-red. Her nose is encrusted with snot, which tells me Tracey hasn't cleaned her in days. In disbelief, I quickly pick her up, cradle her in my arms, and cant, "Bella is such a harmless and beautiful baby. How could anyone hurt her?" doing my best to keep her from crying.

Inside the car, I sit her on my lap and secure the seatbelt around the both of us. But she's still convulsed in cries. To calm her down, I put on some soft music and sing to her. "*Soft and warm, a quiet storm, quiet as when flowers talk at the break of dawn, break of dawn.*" Somehow this eases her into a quieter, if not quite serene, state.

Driving off, I feel so distraught I have to pull over. I've worked hard trying to turn my life around and live as a man of God should, but the Devil is really gunning for me this time, and he's stronger than he's ever been. This is spiritual warfare: I have to fight for my soul. I have to be prepared for anything. *This is my prayer to you, God!* —I cry out.

I drive on. About ten minutes later, I turn down my block. Kendall Drive is normally a quiet one-way, inner-city street, but I see cops cars parked outside my house. Tracey must've called the law after she came to and noticed Bella missing. I stop and hold on tightly to Bella. The best thing is to put the car in reverse and slowly back up, I decide.

Instantly, the sirens blare. Before I even make it to the corner, three cop cars corner me, one coming down the block, the other two heading from an opposite direction. Any other situation and I would have done whatever it took to get away, without a care in the world. But Bella was with me. I had to give up.

Six police officers surround us with their guns trained on us. Tracey lunges out of the farthest patrol car in sight and runs to me yelling, "Give me my baby!" And Bella starts screaming again.

"Place your hands on the staring wheel," orders a muscular black officer with a lazy eye and bald head.

"I have my daughter, sir. Could you please tell your men to put their guns away?" I plead, and slowly position my hands on the staring wheel.

"Everyone, lower your weapons," the officer mandates. "Ma'am, is this your daughter?"

"*Yes!*"

"Sir, I'm going to ask you to unfasten your seatbelt," he says. I obey. He reaches into the car and takes Bella and hands her to Tracey. "Please step out of the car, sir, with your hands on your head." Again, I do as the officer says. A pretty Hispanic policewoman takes my hands, places them behind my back, and handcuffs me.

"I hope you rot in hell, you son of a bitch!" Tracey shrills.

"Not before you," I reply. The policewoman places me in back of the squad car. As we drive away, I catch glimpse of a menacing *Ah-ha-I-gotcha* grin on Tracey's face.

* * *

My appearance before a family-court judge took place two months later. I was dressed in a business-like navy-blue suit, white button-down shirt, navy-blue tie and black leather shoes. I stood mute and holding my composure, because Tracey was in the room and I wanted to choke the life out of her. I refused to make any eye contact with that crazy broad, but I felt her icy glares on me all the time.

"Mr. Daluz, you're here requesting sole custody of your eight-and-a-half-month-old daughter," the judge paraphrased from a document. "I've reviewed your file and I noticed you're a U.S. army veteran. Where did you serve?"

"One year in Fort Sill Oklahoma and two years in Germany, Your Honor."

"Ah. Excellent. I served in Nam myself." I gave the judge

a faint smile and saluted him. The judge saluted me back. "However, can you tell me why you have a criminal record stemming from November 1987, and anything else that you feel is relevant to your case?"

I dropped my head in ignominy. It was an episode I'd tried hard to put behind me and hoped would not be brought up before the court. But my old demons returned with a vengeance.

I had to explain.

- 2 -

November 11, 1987

A year after returning home from Army duty at Fort Sill, at 22 years old, I was sitting in a dark-blue uniform, black sneakers and a black cap inside a tight, stuffy booth on a small island in the middle of a vacant parking lot of a massive Sims warehouse building. On the gray metal desk in front of me lay an old typewriter, on which I was completing a paper on the 1964 Civil Rights movement. In the background, a small and muffled clock radio was playing a song by one of my favorite 1970s Soul groups.

As usual, things were quiet at Sims, my hometown place of employment. This was where they manufactured ink pens and razors, and I had taken a part-time job as a security guard while attending college at Elm City University. Compared to other security gigs I'd worked, in inner-city department stores, this was a piece of cake. In one previous job, for example, I noticed a suspicious-looking young woman walking in and out of the store. I knew she was stealing, but I didn't want to be one of those clowns who mistook being a security guard for policing. I often let people get away with stealing without a word, as long as no one got hurt and other employees or my boss didn't notice. This time, I had to say something, because my supervisor had also seen her carrying bags back and forth but not paying for anything.

I confronted her in front of the store. "Listen, honey, I know what you're doing and I don't want to have you arrested. But you're taking advantage of my kindness. So please, take what you stole and just leave."

"Mind your business, you fake cop!" the woman spewed. Then she stuffed part of a cupcake in her mouth and spit it out on me. Spitting is one of the most degrading things you can do to someone. I didn't react right away. In frustration, I wiped my clothes off and followed her. The woman thief got in her car and stuck the key in the ignition. As she put the car in reverse, I reached into her rolled-down back window and grabbed a bag of chips on the backseat. I ripped open the bag and dumped its contents all over the interior of her car.

"Get the hell out of here, you trick, and don't come back!" I shouted.

As I walked back to the store, though, I suddenly went airborne, flipping backward and the sky above me. I hit the ground hard. The woman's car then raced off. I had just witnessed my first miracle—unknowingly, because I had no personal relationship with God as yet. He allowed me to walk away without a scratch.

Another time, I spotted a tall, really dark black dude with a bald head and nappy beard stuffing cartons of cigarettes into a duffel bag. He was probably in his mid-forties. I approached him. "Hey, you gotta put the bag down and leave," I said.

"F-you. Try and stop me and I'll kill you!" he answered

back. He then pulled out a long knife from his inside coat pocket and threatened to stab me with it. Needless to say, I ran like I had rockets on my shoes. The man chased me out of the store and around the parking lot for several minutes. Eventually, I was able to flag down a police car that happened to be passing by. Its officer came to my aide and arrested the culprit.

Like I said, I didn't have to worry about this type of thing happening at Sims. On this November day, my duties consisted in taking my usual walk through the building to check the perimeters for disturbances. After completing my final check and returning to my stifling cubicle, I shed my jacket, sat down and glanced at the time. The clock said 7:45 p.m. I was 15 minutes away from quitting time. No sooner had I gone back to typing my paper, hoping to put the finishing touches on my report, than the phone sprang to life. On the other end was Chris Thompson, a good friend of mine from high school.

"Section B, this is Michael Daluz. How may I help you?"

"What's up, Mike?" Chris greeted me.

"What's the word, baby boy?" I said excitedly.

"What're you doing after work?"

I looked at the clock again—7:56. I had to punch out at eight. I tore the paper from the typewriter and proudly kissed it. "I'm taking Danielle to dinner to celebrate, 'cause I just finished the best paper of my life," I said to him.

"Congratulations! I don't mean to mess up your plans, but you and Danielle should meet me and Aaron at *Palay's* for a drink," he urged. *Palay's* was a New Haven college bar located on Fitch Street, a quiet street just down the block from the Elm City University campus. It wasn't my normal hangout, but I thought this might give us something different to do.

Besides, maybe Danielle might like to have a drink before we went off to dinner.

Danielle pulled up slowly in front of my booth with her red 1987 Volkswagen Jetta, with its dark-tinted windows. She was 21 years old, a very attractive black female with a gentle shade of caramel, mysterious hazel eyes, soft full lips and long straight hair. She was an only-child of middle class parents, who gave her the finest things. That could have left her spoiled rotten, but she gave them only her best in return. She was a good girl.

I waved at her from my booth. "Look, Danielle's here," I told Chris on the phone. "I can't promise anything, but I'll ask her if she'd like to go."

"Cool. We'll be at *Palay's* at 9 o'clock."

"Ok," I said and hung up.

I gathered my things and climbed into Danielle's car, which had beige leather seats and smelled like raspberries from the dozen or so air fresheners dangling from her rearview mirror. The radio played slow romantic music.

"Hey, baby."

"Hey, honey!" she said, and we kissed. Kissing her always gave me a warm first-love tingle inside. I changed into a white sweat suit and white Addia sneakers and then put on my thick gold chain. Sounds funny now, when I think of it, but that was funky fresh in '87.

"How was it tonight?" she asked cheerily as we pulled off.

I blew sensually in her ear. "Easy...and guess what?"

"What?" Danielle moaned.

"I finished my paper."

"That's excellent," she said, and turned onto I-95 north back to New Haven. Traffic was light.

I reclined in my seat. "It's the best thing I've ever written."

"I'm so proud of you," she said, and blew me a kiss. I reached my hand out as if to catch her kiss then took hold of her hand. "I know I promised we'd spend a quiet evening together, but Chris called to ask if we'd meet him and Aaron at *Palay's* after work. Do you mind hanging out with them tonight?"

Danielle flashed an angry look back. She'd been looking forward to our dinner date for days. "Mike, you said we were gonna go to dinner tonight."

"I know, I'm sorry. I'm just so excited about finishing my paper I need to have a drink and get my groove on. We won't stay long. I promise."

She looked unconvinced. "It's okay. Go have fun with your boys."

"You're not coming in?"

"No. But tomorrow I don't want to hear any excuses. It's you and me, and me and you ONLY."

"Absolutely!"

When we arrived at *Palay's*, people were walking in and out of the joint, hanging outside, or flirting with the opposite sex. Others sat on top of their cars. The air vibrated with the beat of the music every time a patron entered or exited the club.

"Have fun and be safe," Danielle said to me, and gave me a long, hot kiss.

I reached under her car seat and retrieved a .22-caliber semi-automatic pistol, making sure she didn't notice. I concealed it in a holster inside of my coat, under my armpit. Carrying a gun was standard for me. By '87 things had gotten kind of crazy in New Haven. The crack cocaine business was sizzling. Lots of gang violence: Ville vs. KSI, the Tre, the

Jungle, and the Wild Wild West. Each gang fought the other. I was friends with dudes from every area, but I refused to be on the six o'clock news.

I often wonder, if my life would have been different had I just gone to dinner with my girlfriend, or if I hadn't taken that revolver with me. Would I have sorted out the word of God and grown closer to him? Either way, going to that bar on that particular night was my destiny.

I got out of the car and approached Chris and Aaron with high-fives. After some horseplay, I went up to the entrance and was greeted by a large, stonefaced, iron-pumping bouncer, who asked for our personal IDs. We took out our wallets and handed him our cards. He carefully examined them, spending a bit more time on Aaron's, on account of his young looks. As we waited for Aaron's clearance, I peered inside from where I stood. The club was loaded with people dancing, drinking and having a good time.

"Okay," the bouncer muttered, and we all headed straight to the bar. I ordered a round of beers. Immediately, Chris caught sight of six disorderly white guys shooting darts on the opposite side of the club. He leaned over and asked me, as I was bopping my head to the music, "See those white boys over there?"

"Yeah."

Chris, who had the slim, brown-toned features of a male model, sat glaring at them from the dark shadows of the bar with squinting eyes. "One in the middle gettin' ready to shoot the dart? That's Gary Parker. He got me fired from the school dining hall last week. Called me a nigger. I swear I'm gonna knock him out," he told me.

I patted him on his back. "No you're not. You're going to chill and have some fun."

But Chris didn't take one eye off Gary. His knee was shaking like he wanted to rush over to that dude and beat his brains in. He was known for being naive and stubborn. I mean, there were eight or nine guys over there and he was smelling out trouble! I can't really blame him; at 21 years old we all thought we were invincible. But Chris was on the warpath. He wanted *revenge*; I just wanted to have a good time.

I let him wallow in his cloud of anger and scooped out the place. Two female friends from school playing pool were here, Kelly and Kristy. "I'll be back," I said to Aaron and Chris, "Chris, you cool?"

Engrossed with an evil stare, Chris took another swill of his beer. "Yeah, I'm cool." Slowly, I walked over to the pool table, Aaron behind me. When I glanced back, I noticed Chris had ordered a third time, against the bartender's wishes, and was already guzzling it down—without once lifting his eyes from Gary. Predictably, one of Gary's friends noticed his gawking. Gary was a tall, muscular, brash, beer-chugging white dude with brown hair and green eyes. He quickly locked eyes with Chris and flashed a sinister smile.

Meanwhile, Aaron and I went on about Kelly and Kristy. "Damn, Mike, the one with the blond hair is hot!" he whispered in my ear. It was true; Kelly was a beautiful blond. She stood five-feet-two inches tall, had bluish green eyes, and had a perfect body. Not an ounce of fat on her. Kristy was a tall Jamaican girl, who walked very prissy. Years later, she told me she had a crush on me but had never said anything.

"Hey, ladies, how are you? Do you mind if my friend and I join you?" I asked. Of course not, they answered. "Kelly and Kristy, this is Aaron," who answered with a shy, awkward hello.

"Hey, Kelly, you and Aaron are the same major."

"Really? You're studying political science?"

"Yeah, I..." Just as Aaron was about to make his love

connection, we were distracted by some arguing in the background. I turned to see what the commotion was about.

Gary and his pals had just encircled Chris. Without hesitation, Aaron and I tore back. Nineteen years old, Aaron was a short, trim, Italian kid with a muscular build, clipped hairstyle and thin-tipped nose. He had a special place in my heart, because he had the heart of a lion and the spirit of a dove. But the plain fact was that he was the coolest white boy I ever met. He was always himself. He didn't try to act like anyone else or be urbane. He liked to hang around us brothers and he could fight like champ.

"You better get out of my face, buckwheat, or get carried out!" Gary warned Chris.

"Fuck you, white boy!"

"Dude, you're not gonna let this nappy-headed idiot talk to you like that, are you?" one of Gary's companions egged him on.

Gary stepped right into Chris's face. "You talk like you're a big shot, but you ain't nothing but a monkey. Why don't you save yourself the embarrassment and pain and walk away?"

Aaron and I got in between Gary and Chris to try breaking up the confrontation. I yanked Chris by the arm and we both started to walk away.

"You best be lucky your homeboys saved you or I woulda mopped your black ass all over this floor," Gary poked again.

"No, that won't be happening tonight," I insisted.

"Are you sure o' that, tough guy?" another one of Gary's friends chimed in.

"Yeah, I'm quite sure." Nothing was going to happen to Chris if I could help it. Then, the same mountain-sized bouncer that checked our IDs at the door approached me, Chris and Aaron threateningly and asked us to leave the club.

"Why do we have to leave?" I complained. "We weren't the

only ones causing a ruckus! What about them?" The bouncer didn't deign a reply. He just jumped into my face with a stern look and pointed to the door.

"That's cool," I surrendered, his hot anger in my face. If looks could kill, though, the bouncer would have been dead, because I also gave him the deadliest glower in return.

The boys and I made our way down Fitch Street, before deciding to head back to the dorm rooms on the university campus. "I thought you were going to chill out?" I told Chris.

"I'm going to get that white boy."

Aaron—who was often in his own world in a clueless kind of way, but always a loyal friend—said to me, "Mike, that Kelly chick was so hot! Hook me up."

"I heard she's a freak too," I answered. We walked on.

Unexpectedly, Gary's voice rose from across the street. We had no idea Gary and his trouble-seeking chums were trailing us. "*Hey, niggers! What's up, now*?" he shouted. Gary was the ringleader; whatever he said went. His word was gold to his knucklehead buddies, but that was only because he was the rich kid of the bunch.

Chris stopped to stoke the new war of words. "What's up, bitch?" he shouted back, fury in his voice.

"Forget about them. Let's go," Aaron urged him.

"No. Forget *that*. I'm tired of that punk!" Chris declared, and charged across the street.

Not one to back down, Gary ran into the street to meet him in the middle.

"Come on, man, let it go," I hollered. It was too late.

Gary and Chris were literally nose-to-nose. "What you gonna do, nigger?" Gary kept up his steady blurts of the N-word.

Finally, Chris drew his arm so far back—as we used to say when we were kids, "I'll hit you so hard your grandparents will feel it"—and planted one on Gary's face, laying him out on the ground. Seeing this, Gary's friends rushed into the street and pounced on Chris. Aaron and I hurried to his rescue. I didn't want any trouble, but Chris was my friend. And I was both a street fighter and a U.S. soldier, a man whose code of honor held up on the street just as firmly as on the battlefield: *Never leave a man behind.*

So I went to war.

I snatched one kid off Chris and threw a combination of hard punches into his ribs. Aaron tackled another to the ground and proceeded to pound on him mercilessly. I then slammed another kid on top of the hood of a black '85 Thunderbird and beat him senseless. Gary took this chance to creep up behind me and from a side angle smashed me in the nose, shattering it. I collapsed, hitting the pavement hard. After his sneak attack, I realized we were in trouble. The white dudes began to grow in numbers—drunken ones walking down the street and having nothing to do with the fight. They all joined in. We were outnumbered and became separated.

I remember hearing, "Let's kill this nigger." But I couldn't focus after Gary broke my nose. I was still on the ground, everything a blur. Then, I felt a bunch of feet stomping and kicking me. I don't know how many times they hit me. They clearly wanted to kill me. For the first time in my life I blacked out; and yet somehow, I could still hear their laughter and voices ever so slow, as if the batteries in the tape recorder were dying.

"How you feeling, tough guy?" one dude shouted. "I can't hear you. Speak up," another prodded. When I regained consciousness, just for a moment, one of them was shaking me, and then a hail of fists rained on me.

That was when it hit me like a light. I had a revolver!

I used what little life I had left in me to reach for it. I pulled it out and aimed. At whom I had no idea. I really couldn't see anything. My hands shook so bad I thought I was going to drop the gun. I pulled the trigger. Nothing happened.

"The gun's fake!" Gary's henchmen shouted.

"Pick him up," ordered Gary. The goons obeyed. I held on to my gun, now struggling to switch the safety switch to fire. I didn't want to kill anyone, but indescribable fear had gripped me, and I had to do what I had to do for sheer survival.

I fired. Someone screamed so loud it could've quickened the dead.

Our attackers panicked and scattered like dust in the wind. I tried to run too, but I fell in a pile of leaves. A few seconds later Chris and Aaron, badly injured themselves—though nowhere near as bad as I—came to my side and lifted me to my feet. They were shocked: my face was unrecognizable.

"Mike...I'm so sorry!" Chris cried out in a quavering voice.

"We gotta get him to a hospital," Aaron said.

"And say what? We were mugged and he shot a white boy? We'll go to jail! No, what we have to do is get Mike back to the dorm rooms and figure this thing out."

Chris and Aaron dragged me down the long deserted road. The campus was only five minutes away, but it felt like we were walking forever. A few cars slowed down for a second or two of live entertainment and rode on by.

"I'm hurtin'. Let me...try to walk on my own," I muttered in pain. Chris and Aaron struggled to stand me straight on my feet. I took two steps forward, as cautiously as I could, but almost plummeted to the concrete. They caught my fall, perched my arms on their shoulders and we resumed our trek down the orange-lit street.

- 3 -

At the dorms, Chris and Aaron brought me to the back emergency exit doors, where they knew no one would be hanging around. While Chris went to open the door, Aaron eased me down on the ground against the wall. The door was locked.

"Stay here with Mike," Chris told Aaron. "I'll go through the front lobby and open the door for y'all." He crept around to the front of the building hoping to avoid bumping into anyone. Meanwhile, I was feeling colder and colder. It felt like pneumonia setting in. The violent events of the last two hours played over and over again in my mind, like a broken record. Then I heard the voices of Ted Miller, Tre Blackmon, Eric Gonzales, Wayne Porter and a few other guys, all members of an off-campus multicolor brotherhood calling itself F-troop, of which I too was a member.

Ted Miller was an attractive, caramel-skinned black guy with a chipped front tooth but a body like that of a wide receiver, muscles ripping everywhere. He wore his hair low and wavy. Tre Blackmon was a tall, lean fellow with flawless midnight skin and big feet. His shoes looked like tug boats, and he had big hand. For some reason, he was the ladies favorite. Wayne Porter was a class unto himself. A nineteen-year-old brown, baby-faced, stubby brother, he groomed his hair in the typical Hip Hop style of the eighties—flattop and hair shaved on the sides—but dressed like Bob Hope, ascot and all. While everyone else was listening to Hip Hop, Wayne was heavily into Frank Sinatra and Elvis Presley. All these guys were my brothers and I loved them. When they saw me slumped in the corner, they couldn't believe their eyes.

Eric—a smooth playboy-type Hispanic who thought he was Hugh Hefner walking around the dorms in a robe and slippers—crouched down and gently hugged me. "Wake up, Mike," he pleaded. I didn't budge, because for a second time I was going out for the count.

"He looks terrible. Why didn't you bring him to the hospital?" Wayne pried.

"Because Mike shot one of 'em. Gary Parker, and he might be dead," Chris whispered.

"He what?" Eric asked in alarm.

"Chill. Everybody just take it easy and help me get him upstairs."

There was no time to bicker, so the guys just cooperated with Chris. They lifted me up, Aaron holding the door open, and carried me up three flights of stairs. When we reached the third floor, he peeked into the hallway. "We're clear." They rushed me into room 325, which I recall being very small. There was a single twin-sized bed, small bathroom, tight closet, desk with pens and papers, computer and telephone on it. They laid me on the bed, where I began to cough up blood.

Wayne frantically paced back and forth. Tre punched his fist into his hand and asked, "Where are those punks?"

"Everybody just calm down," said Chris.

"Hell no! Look at our boy. We can't just sit here and do nothing. We gotta find those crackers," Ted shouted.

"Yo, I agree," Eric said.

"No. We have to get Mike out of these clothes, clean him up and figure out our next move."

Growing up in a household full of women and a stepfather I thought hated my guts really made me cherish each and every one of these guys. They say when you're having a near-death experience, your life flashes in front of you. I fell into unconsciousness again and had a flashback.

I was 13 years old. My baseball team had just won the finals and we advanced to play in the state championship. I was so proud I couldn't wait to get home to tell my parents...Bursting through the front door, dressed in a dirty New Haven Knights baseball uniform, I shouted through the living room, "Mom, pop! We won, we won!" Then, "Mom—pop?" Not a sound. The house seemed empty.

Finally, I heard laughter coming from the den, which was in the far rear of the house. I ran over as fast as I could. My mother was sitting on the couch watching television, my stepfather, Curtis—I called him Pop—and my two little stepsisters, Jackie and Stacey, were having the time of their lives. They all sat on the floor building a larger-than-life dollhouse.

"We won!" I yelled out again.

"Move," my mother yelled. I had inadvertently blocked her view of the television screen.

Her uncaring response didn't faze me, at first. I just hopped out of her view and again announced, "Pop, pop, we won!" But Pop was thoroughly engrossed in what he was doing.

His affections usually went to my stepsisters, his biological daughters. Cute little girls they were, but very spoiled and vindictive. You see, Pop put them on a pedestal, while constantly saying negative things about me. He had turned everyone in the house, including my big sister Brenda, against me. He had them believe that I was a bad kid, as if by an evil spell. Pop had been raising me since the age of two, but why he didn't like me was a complete mystery to me. Maybe it was because I looked exactly like my real father. He couldn't stand my real father, who was a pretty boy. It's also possible that Curtis secretly wished he'd fathered me himself? Up to that point, I had both feared and respected him. Not anymore.

"Pop," I called for recognition a third time.

"What?" he hollered.

"I hit two home runs and I made MVP! Are you gonna come to my championship game next week?"

"Don't you see I'm busy. What's wrong with you?" he said.

Dejected, I plumped down on the sofa next to my mother, who just as quickly turned her nose up at me and inched away.

I was sweaty and filthy. Noticing this, Pop roared, "Get off of my furniture with your dirty clothes." I just about leaped out of my skin coming off that sofa. "Boy, the lawn needs to be cut. Handle that right now," he ordered. I felt small and insignificant.

"You heard what your father said—do it," my mother seconded.

It felt like abject defeat watching Pop and my stepsisters interacting, while all I managed to attract were negative remarks—even when I was accomplishing good things. I reacted by isolating myself from my family. I wanted nothing to do with them...

* * *

When I came to on the dorm bed, I realized the guys had changed me into tight yellow sweet pants, a green sweater and a pair of old black sneakers. Before blacking out again, I saw Aaron put my bloody clothes and jacket in the closet, and Ted peering out the window.

"Damn, the cops are here!" said Ted. Chris sped to the window to see for himself. An army of police vehicles had swarmed in below.

"Guys! Don't panic." Tre got up and headed for the door. I had no idea what he was about going to do, but whatever it was I was confident it would be brilliant. He had always been a rebel ready to suffer any consequences for a good cause.

"Hey, where are you going?" Wayne asked.

"I don't know. All I know is that we have to get Mike out of here and take him to the hospital." Chris grabbed Tre by the arm to stop him. Tre pulled away. "Get the hell off me! Look at Mike. He needs a doctor!"

"Come on, guys. Now is not the time to be arguing," I heard Eric say. Ted agreed. There was a knock at the door. "Who is it?" Chris asked.

"It's C." "C" was Calvin Merrit, better known as Crazy Legs, because he had long pencil-like legs and ran track. Chris opened the door and let him in quickly. "The cops are in the building and they're searching the rooms. You gotta get Mike out of here."

"Let's go. Get him up," Chris directed.

"Mike. Mike. Come on, man, get up. We have to get you out of here," Eric said, softly nudging me. I moaned and groaned, as the guys carefully lifted and rushed me out of the room and toward the elevator that would send us up to the third floor. Ted pressed a button on the wall. A few anxious moments later, while we waited for the elevator, two Caucasian officers spotted "C" and charged down the hall. "Stop!" one of them hollered. I still recall their names—Officers Malone and Duffy.

We were trapped. There was no way my brothers could outrun the cops while carrying me. But Tre had an idea. He reached over and pulled the fire alarm, which instantly blared so loud it almost caused the windows to crack. In seconds, students flooded the hallway. Officers Malone and Duffy tried to squeeze through the confused throng, but we managed to get into the elevator and ride it down to the lobby. There, we blended into the sea of youth.

We were all on edge. The police were ordering everyone to exit the building. In the parking lot, they separated everyone: white kids on one side, black females on the other, black males in a straight line in the middle of the street. All told, there were about thirty-five of us. The cops ordered us to stand, as if in boot camp, so that they, together with the white boys, could get a good look at us. The street was calm, no traffic. But the night was turning brisk and I was in excruciating pain. Moments later, Malone and Duffy joined Sergeant Klein, who marched up and down our line like a drill sergeant. In no time they started to question each one of us.

"Were you involved in the shooting?" Sergeant Klein shouted at Craig Nelson.

Craig was a burly linebacker on the university football team and, before this night, he and I didn't get along. But he kept quiet, smacked his gum with an attitude and blew a bubble.

"Sir, spit the gum out," Malone said with an air of disgust. Craig cooperated. "Now, were you involved in the shooting?"

"Na," Craig replied in a husky voice as brawn as his stature.

By then everyone on campus had heard about the shooting. I used to be very popular on campus, known for getting the finest ladies, scoring grades at the top of my class and owning two lethal hands. Being the big dude on campus earned me lots of enemies, but some of those enemies stood in line with me right now, Craig among them. I had stolen his girlfriend during my freshmen year. It wasn't like I wanted her. She pursued me. Tonight, though, we all put our differences aside and stood united as brothers of color.

One of the white attackers noticed me and pointed to where I stood farther down the line. Just as Officer Malone was moving towards me, Craig created a diversion by punching the white kid in the face. This triggered a fight, but Malone, Duffy, Sergeant Klein and the other cops quickly got a handle on the situation and arrested Craig. I was passed down the line. In the midst of the chaos, a second white kid identified me, "That guy over there wearing the yellow sweat pants. He's the shooter," he said accusingly.

Eric was standing only a few steps away from the guy who dropped the dime on me. He rushed out of line and punched him in the back of the head like a ton of bricks. A second brawl erupted, and in the chaos I was once more passed to the end of the lineup.

"We got your back, Mike. We ain't gonna let these pigs get you," a black students assured me. I didn't know him, but he kept me on my feet.

"Thank you, dog," Michael said. Sergeant Klein, fed up with our charades, finally got everyone's attention by firing his pistol in the air. "Gentlemen. We can play this game all night, but everyone here will go to jail. That's a promise! Do I make myself clear?"

Seeing the cops take the guys into custody made me decide to turn myself in. I was grateful for what my friends and brothers alike were doing for me, but I was a man who stood on his own. I couldn't let others take the fall. I stumbled out of line clutching my stomach.

At once, I was apprehended with guns pointing from every side. Malone's face was red as a tomato when he grabbed me. "Lay on the ground!" he shouted, and forced me down to my knees. He handcuffed me and read me my rights. Another officer stuffed me in back of a squad car. No one cared about my injuries.

At the sight of my treatment, the other black students started to riot. "*The police is the devil! The police is the devil! The police is the devil!*" bellowed the crowd.

"You have no idea who you're messing with, boy," Malone whispered in my ear inside the squad car.

As he drove away, with Officer Duffy in the passenger seat, I looked out the window at my friends pounding on their chest. They were charged with deep feelings, and threw up the peace sign. Some of them chased the car for a distance and cast sticks, rocks and whatever they could find.

"You feel good about yourself, pal?" Duffy asked me.

"No, I don't. I need to go to the hospital." They just looked at each other and laughed. "Officers. I shot that man in self-defense. Do you see me? I was almost beaten to death!"

"Look, calm down," Malone said.

"Calm down? I need to see a doctor!"

Malone glanced into the rearview mirror and shot me a wise smirk. "Hey, did you see the game Sunday?" Duffy asked him.

"Nope, the wife had me out shopping all day."

I started to suffocate. "Can I have some water, please?"

Duffy cut me off and resumed his conversation with Malone. "You missed a kickass game," then turned to me and smiled. "No pun intended."

"You're an asshole, you know that?" Malone jokingly said to his partner. Again they chuckled.

Instead of taking me to the hospital, they had decided to return to the scene of the crime. It was now 3 a.m. and the streets were dead. When we got there, Duffy stepped out of the vehicle and snatched me out harshly. He flicked on his flashlight and shone it straight into my face. "Find the gun," he demanded.

I held up my hands to block the light. "Find *what*?" I asked.

He pushed me into a pile of leaves. "The gun!" he said, while Malone seated himself on the hood of the car and lit a cigarette.

"I need to go to the hospital."

"You're not going anywhere until you find that gun," he warned.

Malone looked on menacingly. He blew some more smoke in the air, then decided to chuck the cigarette on the ground and crush it with his heel. He reached inside the car and grabbed his flashlight resting on the front seat. He approached a dumpster next to the squad car, flaring his flashlight inside.

"Hey, you, get over here," he ordered. I crawled through the leaves on my hands and knees, and looked up at him. I had to fight to get on my feet. As I lurched over to the garbage dumpster, he said, "I have a feeling the gun's in there."

"With all due respect, officer, I'm not getting in there."

"You hear that? He's not getting in there. I guess he's too

good to get dirty," Duffy said and dove into the dumpster. I wanted to say shut the hell up, but I was in enough trouble already; so I kept my mouth shut.

"Either you get in there or you go to jail," Malone threatened.

"Then take me to jail."

- 4 -

My gun was never found. I thought I had dropped it accidentally in the leaves but I honestly could not remember what I did with it. I was taken to Union Avenue police station, located in an area of New Haven we called the Wild Wild West—so named because gunfights seemed to take place every day, just like in an old Western. Unlike Westerns, though, the showdowns didn't happen only at high noon. It didn't matter what time of day; bullets were flying.

The police station was like any other: criminals being booked, telephones ringing nonstop, fax machines and typewriters chugging endlessly. They processed me and put me in a cell with twenty-five other guys. As Duffy opened the bullpen, I recognized most of my friends. It was as if I'd walked in on a party. Chris looked petrified, but very glad to see me. I was later informed that my F-troop brother Ted and once-upon-a-time enemy Craig were taken to the station but quickly released. I also saw guys I hadn't seen in years—Sam Hunts for one. Sam was a good person, but he was off-the-wall. Cross him and he'd put a bullet in you at the drop of a dime. The hardest thugs in the city wouldn't mess with him. He and I had met when I was 14 and Sam was around 18.

That had been right after I lost interest in baseball and my parents wrote me off. Yeah, I still lived under their roof now, but there was no relationship; they only communicated with me to tell me to do some slave work around the house and yard, or just to make me feel like two cents. We lived in an upper middle-class neighborhood and a decent house. The backyard had a few acres of trees. The spring before I had started to rebel, Pop made me cut down all the trees in the backyard, exactly fifteen trees. It was exhausting work. Had he done it to teach me the responsibilities of a man, I would have taken it. But that wasn't it at all. He did it to keep me under his tight grip. He ruled with an iron fist, literally. Up to that point I'd been a good kid, no thanks to him. Then, one day he made me stand in the corner. Just a couple of steps in front of me, he began pitching apples at my head and forehead for amusement. I decided then that I was no longer going to take it. After that I began to hang out in the streets and took part in petty crime with my friends.

Anyway, Sam was the big man around my neighborhood and younger hustlers like me looked up to him and his boy, Big H. They recognized that I was a tough kid and soon put me down with their crew. They became the big brothers I never had. I was a teen deep in the streets and acting the fool. Finally, at 17 and in full-blown rebellion, I clearly couldn't live under the same roof as Pop any longer, so my mother forced me to enlist in the army, thinking that if I didn't leave I would die in those streets or go to jail.

When I entered the service I had no idea what I was getting into. At the enlisting station the recruiting officer told me I had scored exceptionally high, which meant I could always avoid combat and instead work in the hospital. But, he explained, if I did take that position I would be considered weak. He suggested I join a combat-arms M.O.S., as that would bring me honor.

I wanted nothing more than respect and honor. I signed on to become a U.S. Army artillery "red-leg."

Soon after joining I ran afoul of military authority. I had no previous idea how much power and control a drill sergeant had over subordinates. I rebelled, disobeying orders and getting into altercations. I had brought the streets with me into the army, and got charged for my negative behavior. In time, I began to surrender to authority and in effect became a trained, disciplined killer. After my tour of duty, I received an honorable discharge, just as the recruiting officer said I would. Respect and honor were all I wanted; only, it took me little time to live out my mother's nightmare, drawing ever closer to prison.

When I entered the cell that day, bloodied and defeated, Sam was rolling dice with brothers who came from another seedy section of New Haven called the Island. "Oh, my God! Is that little Mike Daluz?" he called out, and stood up and hugged me. But I was in too much pain to embrace him back. "I heard what happened," he said.

"How did you hear about it?" I mumbled feebly.

"It's all over the news! They said you got into a beef with some white boys in *Palay's* and just started shooting up the crackers."

"That's not what happened," I replied.

Seeing how I was in no physical shape to stand, let alone talk, he shot one look at five dudes sitting on the bench and whispered, "Get your asses up! My little brother needs to lay down!"

Without a word, they jumped off the bench. Sam and Chris helped me to the seat, where I crawled into a ball. Sam then ran to the bars of the cell and, gripping them tightly, yelled out, "Yo, get a doctor in here for my little brother." I drifted off to sleep.

The next day a hefty police officer came to the bullpen door and opened it. "Chris Thompson, you made bail," he announced. Chris, who lay on the floor, sprang up like a frog and came over to me. "Mike, wake up!" I opened my eyes to him. "Mike, I made bail," he uttered somberly. I guess he was glad to be getting out of there, but he didn't want to leave me. "I'm going to make sure you get out of here and let everyone know what really happened."

"I have to use my phone call to contact my mother," I told him. "As soon as you leave, call Danielle and tell her where I am."

"You got it, Mike."

"Thompson. Let's go!" the cop rushed him. Chris hugged me and exited the cell.

About an hour later I was taken out of the holding cell and led down the hall to get fingerprinted. Here I was before this old white policeman in his late sixties, the skin of his face looking like it had moon craters in it. He probably should have been in a senior-citizens home, not on the force. He stared at me with outrage in his eyes. I didn't care. I was the victim here, so I stared back at him without blinking once.

I was soon standing in a long line waiting to make my phone call. Cooling my heels, I thought about last night. I was angry about everything, but especially because I wouldn't have ended up here had I spent a quiet evening with Danielle. I was also furious that neither Gary Parker nor any of the other white boys were charged or arrested for attacking us. I found myself wishing I'd killed them all. A feeling of pure hatred for white people overcame me.

Finally, it was my turn to use the phone. I decided to call my parents for help. I picked up the phone and dialed. My mother answered. "Hello," I said dejectedly, "Ma, I'm in jail," I announced, and waited for a response. "Did you hear what happened?"

"Yes, I heard. It's all over the news," she answered. She didn't seem all that concerned. I heard my stepfather's voice hollering in the background. "*Yeah, jailbird, we heard!*" I blocked out his comments and kept talking. "Ma, whatever the news is saying about me, don't believe it. Tomorrow I need you to find me a lawyer." I could hear Pop rushing her off the phone. "Ma, why did you let Pop treat me the way he did when I was a kid? And why do you let him to run all over you now?

"Please. Not now, Michael. Anyways, your father's handling everything. I have to go. Your father and I are going to dinner," she blithely said, followed by the dead tone of the phone. My own mother had just hung up in my face! I was crushed. That hurt more than the beating I had taken. I stood motionless and stunned, unable to comprehend my parents' lack of emotions.

A few moments later, I was escorted back to the bullpen. Sam was still in there, of course. He and I sat and talked for hours catching up on everyone from around the way. It turned out he was locked up for drug possession, which didn't surprise me. Sam was a big-time hustler in New Haven. When I got out and ever needed a job, he offered, I could see his partner and my other big brother Big H. I laughed at the idea. The Army changed me, I answered. I wasn't the lost kid I once used to be.

A week went by. I was still locked up at Union Avenue police station. Then, one day the remaining prisoners and I were shackled by our wrists, ankles and waists. We were put into a bus and herded into court. By then I had talked to my parents again. Pop was taking his sweet time about hiring me a lawyer, I guess to teach me another lesson: this time for having my face beat in and defending myself. As we entered the courtroom, we were seated in the front row of the court. I was surprised to see the courtroom filled with my friends from school—Tre, Ted, Wayne, Eric, all my F-Troop brothers, and Danielle. They were so excited to see me they all stood up and applauded.

Danielle, who was bawling her eyes out, ran forward to give me a hug, but the courtroom guards stopped her. I told her to calm down and that everything would be fine. Judge Thomas McClain stepped out of his chambers with a lazy I-can't-wait-to-get-this-over-with expression. Everyone fell silent and rose. When he took his place on the bench, we all sat down.

Meanwhile I had no lawyer. Instead, I had to represent myself. But I wasn't too worried. Not at first. I was confident that, after taking note of my injuries and hearing my case, the judge would find me innocent.

"Docket number 12, State v. Michael Daluz, approach the bench," Judge McClain stated. I did, behind me a courtroom full of friends, who dutifully rose with me and burst again in applause. "Quiet! Everybody sit down! This is not a concert," the judge shouted, banging his gavel.

I turned to Danielle to comfort her. I lipped to her the words, "Everything's gonna be all right," though deep down I didn't really believe that.

"In the case of docket number 12," the prosecutor began, "the charges against Michael Daluz are attempted murder."

"Mr. Daluz, how do you plead?"

"Not guilty."

"Mr. Daluz, your bail is set at $165,000."

The courtroom gasped. I couldn't believe either the amount or the charge of attempted murder. I shut my eyes and gnashed my teeth. My chest felt as if it had caved in. How was I going to find the bail money? I couldn't go to my parents; it would be like telling them they were right about their son, the screw-up. Still, I had no choice. I had to ask them. I pondered the idea, as the marshal took me away.

In the end, I spent three weeks waiting to be bailed out of Union Avenue police station. I called my parents countless times, leaving messages about the bail. Not once did they answer their phone. In the end, it was Danielle's mother who came to my rescue. She went into her family's bank savings account and got me out of jail.

I was very thankful, but saddened at the same time. A stranger was by my side while, once again, my family denied me their support. That was when I vowed I would never speak to my parents again.

- 5 -

December 19, 1987

One more week before Christmas break. The midterms were in session. While everyone else was preparing to leave campus for the holidays, I faced possibly twenty years of prison time and certain expulsion from school. My entire academic future lay in the hands of University Dean Grayson—an old, cold-hearted, by-the-book white man who reminded me of Alfred Hitchcock. The black students always felt his antipathy so clearly he could have worn it on his sleeve. Nevertheless, I was permitted to write my exams. I recall the embarrassment. I felt like the most dangerous criminal in history pulling into the main campus parking lot of Cedar Hall.

It wasn't much different from that night I had been hauled off in a cop car after of my attack, and the only way I could return to school was in handcuffs and a police escort. As I walked down the halls, people pointed at me in whispers, some laughing. The black students applauded, as if I was some sort of hero. It was all so overwhelming. The cops brought me inside an empty closed-in room with nothing but a desk. It smelled stale. On top of the desk was my ten-page psychology exam, a pencil and two sheets of scrap paper.

One of the officers removed the cuffs. I sat down.

It wasn't easy concentrating with two policemen standing over me, but somehow I pulled through. I completed the exam in less than half the allotted time. One thing about me, regardless of what I might have turned into, in or out of the streets, I've always had intelligence. The only thing that stumped me was the fact that I'd gotten myself into such a mess. With all the wrongs I had committed while growing up and never got caught for, my life lay in ruins because I had simply decided to protect myself.

When I was done, the policemen marched me straight to Dean Grayson's office. The moment of truth had arrived. As soon as I entered his office, gaping at the mercilessness on his face, I knew I was screwed. I'd shot a white kid. No matter what else had happened that night, I shot a *white kid*. And not just any white kid. I later learned that Gary Parker was the son of a police officer for another Connecticut town.

I moved to take a seat.

"No need to sit down, this won't take long," Grayson curtly said. "I've concluded that you are a danger to everyone on this campus, and have decided to have you permanently removed."

"With all due respect, sir, I am a U.S. Army vet, and I had to protect myself. I had to save my life."

"I'm sorry but you must leave this campus immediately."

"Please don't do this, sir. All I have is my education."

"You should have thought of that when you chose to take the course of action that you did. Officers, take him out of here."

The cops grabbed me and started to move me out of Grayson's office.

"Sir, please reconsider. I'm very remorseful for what happened and I will do whatever it takes to prove it. Put me on academic probation if you have to, but please don't expel me!"

"I'm sorry; that's my decision. Officers—"

Unable to except his answer, I lost control for a split second. I pushed both cops off me and stood pounding my fist on his desk. "I am not gonna let you take my life from me!"

Dean Grayson didn't flinch. He was confident I wasn't going to do anything drastic. He just slumped back in his chair and lamped at me. "So, that's how you show you're 'remorseful', huh? Officers, get this thug out of my sight." My educational and public record was in shambles.

Being a menace to society, I had decided, why not act out the role. There was no turning back. For the next month or so I was in and out of court. I was also getting drunk and smoking lots of weed. Plenty of times I stood before the judge intoxicated, which didn't help matters.

Then came the day I received my sentence. On March 17, 1988, the judge sentenced me to eighteen months for attempted murder and I had six months to turn myself in to the authorities. Eighteen months for *attempted murder!* It was a far cry from the twenty years I expected, almost an admission that I shouldn't be given any time at all, and that I'd shot Gray Parker in self-defense.

I was really despondent, to the point where I wanted to kill myself, along with anybody who said anything to me I didn't like or who looked at me the wrong way. White people especially. My parents didn't seem to care what happened to me. Even some friends started to shun me, so I gave in to self-pity and kept making excuses for myself. After sentencing, I threw my hands up and walked away from reality.

One day, I took a bus into the Hamilton street projects, a dangerous section of town. The projects were rundown and surrounded by a high, black metal gate built to protect the low-income families that lived there, it was thought. My best guess was that the gate kept them caged in so they'd get comfortable with their surroundings and stop wanting to better themselves. Maybe they could just kill each other off.

I opened the gate and passed through into what looked like a different world. People packed the courtyard—hanging out, smoking and drinking, playing cards. Folks were arguing; music blasted amid random drug transactions. There were children playing hide-and-go-seek, little girls skipping rope, babies crying and walking around barefoot or in their pampers. The Hamilton Street Projects was truly chaotic. The street was very long, going for about a mile and finishing at a dead end. Cars were parked up and down.

Walking through the courtyard, I quickly bumped into old friends. Then I heard this deep, raspy voice shout my name across the yard from behind. "Yo, Michael!"

I turned around. It was Big H, Sam's boy. He was like a big brother to me. He came sprinting over, and we embraced. I felt nothing but genuine love from this guy.

"My God, if it isn't my little brother Mike! What's going on with ya? Haven't seen you in what, four or five years?"

"Yeah, that's about right. I haven't seen you since I left for the Army."

"So how *was* the army?"

I gazed into his eyes. "It changed me—a lot."

"That's cool," Big H stood back a few steps, looking me up

and down and smiling. He held his arms out wide. "Look at you, Mike, you're a grown man!"

We hugged again.

"Come on, let me show you off to everybody who ain't seen you in awhile."

He put his arm around my neck and paraded me around the project. I was a star that day. It was like a homecoming and I was back in the mindless jungle, I thought to myself. From that point I was a fixture on the streets—or the whipping boy who did the Devil's dirty work.

* * *

Two and a half months after my expulsion from school, I had to ask my grandmother if I could live with her for a while, because my parents wouldn't let me near their house. Grams lived in a three-family, bluish-gray fixer upper located on a small, dull street, which seemed to be hidden from the world even though it was smack-dab in the middle of the ghetto. The old-school Cape Verdean woman named Lillian Daluz, whom I called her Grams, wasn't the most affectionate woman in the world. No sugar cookies and milk waiting on the table when you came over; no kisses all over your face at the sight of you. She did lots of yelling, though. I couldn't blame her for hollering all the time: there were nineteen of us grandchildren. Sometimes we'd stay at her house all at the same time. Another major reason for her hard exterior was her strict upbringing. She was the daughter of a man who had come from Portugal while a teenager. In his early thirties, he had to struggle to make ends meet with two children and a wife in his charge. After my great grandmother passed away, Grams became the oldest of the family, but she was still left with all the work. She acted as both sister and woman of the house.

I can't say that living with her was a pleasant experience.

I remember the day I arrived at her place. Standing in front of the gate holding a large trash-bag filled with my belongings, I looked up at the second floor window to see if she was looking out. She was always gazing out of that window. She wasn't there this time, so I stepped onto the porch, with a great deal of hesitation. I really didn't need to hear more criticism from anybody.

Finally, after rehearsing what I'd say to her, I rang the bell. Moments later, wearing a long night robe and rollers in her hair, she opened the door. I had my head down.

As I shifted my eyes up at her, she didn't look happy to see me. "Hey, Grams, how you doing?" I said.

"I was sleep. What do you need?" she coldly asked.

"Grams, I need a place to stay."

"Jesus! You kids think my house is a hotel. How long, Michael?"

"Just until October."

Grams sighed heavily then stepped aside, leaving the door open for me. I entered. "Thanks, Grams," I said, and kissed her on the cheek as I walked past.

"Just don't get comfortable."

"I'll only be here for a few months."

"You got that right, because I'm tired o' you kids runnin' in an' out of my house every time you get into trouble."

Gram's house was frayed but clean. The roof needed fixing. The living room floor was covered with stained beige carpeting, two sunken-in brown micro-fabric sofas and a sturdy, outdated, 32-inch oak television that sat on the floor. I dropped my bag next to the television before plopping on the couch.

"Uh, uh, you're not sleeping on *my* couch," she said and pointed to the floor. "*That's* your bed."

"Come on, Grams, how am I gonna sleep on that hard floor?"

"Figure it out. I'm going back to bed."

She returned to her room and shut the door. I lay down on the floor, where I slept for the night. I had four months left before being locked away for a while. Hell, I had to do what I had to do to survive.

* * *

The next day was rainy. I was sitting on the passenger's side of Big H's black Mercedes Benz. The tinted windows were rolled up and the car was filled with smoke as Big H and I passed a blunt ("weed") back and forth. We were scooping out the scene waiting for our usual customers: night crawlers and fiends in need of their daily medication.

A big-boned, brown-skinned woman dressed provocatively but filthily staggered over to my side of the car, soaking wet. She knocked on the window, which I lowered with a stern glare in my eyes. No words were exchanged. The woman, looking extremely anxious, handed me a fist full of wrinkled, wet dollar bills. I counted them. After I handed her a tiny capsule of crack cocaine, she sped-walked down the street with a rotten swagger and she was off to the races.

The corner I hustled on was Grand Avenue and Ferry Street. A gang of us stood on that block day and night—the street expression for that was "hugging the block." One specific episode stands out in my mind. One humid night, a rundown 1980 Volkswagen approached us slowly. The driver looked suspicious to me and my boys. He was a sickly looking white guy in his mid- to late forties with thick glasses and greasy black hair.

"Hey, anybody got some blow?" he asked.

"What? Beat bricks, white boy!" one of my companions said.

This seemed to frighten him, so he started to drive away. But I needed this sell and I was determined to get it. I couldn't let him get away. I ran after the car. "Hey, wait," I yelled out. He pulled over to the curb.

"Yo, Mike, chill—that clown could be police!"

"Naw, he's cool. I got this baby." I jogged over to the car and stuck my head into the passenger's window and eyed him. His complexion was a burning red. "How much you spending?" I asked the driver.

"In the ball park of three to four hundred," he replied, stuttering terribly.

I tried to open the door, but the door was locked. The man didn't seem to want me getting in his car and it riled me. But then I wasn't about to do a transaction in the open like that. "Open the door," I demanded. His hands shook something awful as he reached over and unlocked the door. I hopped in. "You're not a cop are you?"

"Oh, absolutely not!" the man said, skittishly fixing his glasses.

"Then relax," I said, still incensed. "Take a left at this corner." I took him into the Hamilton Street Projects. We drove to the end of the dead-end road. "Pull over."

Looking around with wide eyes, the driver did what I told him to do. "So you got the blow?"

"Don't worry about that. Show me the money first."

The man dug in his pocket and retrieved a stack of crisp hundred-dollar bills. Something possessed me. As he counted the money, I punched my customer in the face repeatedly then drew my 9mm pistol from my right-side pocket and pointed it at his head. "Get the fuck out of the car!" I ordered softly.

"Please don't shoot me. You can have the money!"

"I don't want your money. Just get out of the car."

He began to cry about his children and wife. I didn't care about any of that. I was filled with too much hate. I opened my door and yanked him out. He hit the pavement with a thud. I stood over him aiming the gun right between his eyes. The man groveled on like a petrified dog about to be scolded by its master. I felt really powerful and fulfilled.

"Come on, man, don't hurt me please!"

"Shut up! I'm gonna make you feel how I felt when y'all took my life from me."

I cocked back the gun then slowly proceeded to squeeze the trigger. Just then, I noticed an ancient-looking black man with long, nasty-looking dreadlocks and an artificial leg standing across the street glowering gravely at me. It caused me to freeze for a second. The old man dug in his shopping cart filled with bottles and cans and took out a cardboard sign. He held the sign up high. VENGEANCE IS MINE SAID THE LORD it read in big bold letters.

It was the strangest thing. I wasn't sure if what I was seeing was real or not. *What's going on?*

I had a change of heart about murdering the driver.

"Get up!" I yelled, keeping my eye on the wanderer across the street. My captive wasted no time scuttling to his feet and running to his car.

That was the second time I had witnessed a vision from God. Though I didn't immediately recognize it as one, the old man mesmerized me. I watched him limp away with his cart, which had a loud squeaky wheel. Down the street he pushed until I could see him no more.

I recall looking up to the sky and bawling my eyes out. I didn't understand why I was here. I put the gun to my own head. But I didn't have the guts to pull the trigger. I let two shots in the air.

"*What the hell do you want from me?*" my voice echoed across the street.

- 6 -

"Rob, open the door. It's Mike!" I demanded.

By then my old handsome, "lady's man" persona had turned into a mangy and desperate monster that had no concept of sleep, let alone proper habits in food, health or morals. But I just didn't give a damn anymore. Getting high became my religion. I was pretty bad off.

I leaned against the door. Rob was an associate with whom I used to get high and whom I'd gotten out of a lot of trouble, along with other dealers I happened to be close with. "Rob, open the damn door—it's Mike!" I could hear movements and voices on the other side of the door. Still no answer. I pounded the door to no end, determined to get inside. "I know you're in there, I can hear you. Open the door."

"Come back later, I'm busy."

"I can't 'come back later.' I have to go to Bridgeport and get this money June-bug owes me."

Robbed opened and stuck his head out.

"I need a ride. I'll hit you with a few dollars."

"What's a few dollars?"

"Two hundred. I shouldn't have to give you nothing. All the shit I got you out of!"

He opened the door all the way. I stepped inside and stood by the door. The kitchen was the first room you entered coming into Rob's apartment. It was tightly spaced and grimy—dishes piled to the ceiling, filthy floor, plastic bags in the corner overflowing with trash. So many roaches crawled on the counter tops that if Rob had offered me a glass of water I wouldn't have accepted it. Two other characters I'd never seen before sat at the kitchen table: a Hispanic woman in her late twenties and a black dude twice her age.

The girl held a lighter in one hand and a crack pipe in the other. She put the lighter up to the end of the pipe and attempted to light it, but it wouldn't ignite. In frustration she tried a few more times without success.

"Hurry up, baby!" her sugar-daddy shouted.

"Stop playing around with our shit!" Rob piped in.

"*Your* shit? This ain't your shit. Keep fucking with me, you won't get nothin'," the girl replied.

The girl's boyfriend grabbed her arm to pry the pipe out of her hand, but she held on to it for dear life. "Get off of me, Country!" she shouted. Then "Country" overpowered his "hoe-in-training" and ripped the pipe out of her hand. I say ripped because he broke her skin. "Ouch! You cut me," she hollered.

"Shut up!" he barked, and lit the pipe.

I looked back at Rob. "So this is why you didn't want me to come in, huh?" I told him. "You were having a party and didn't invite me."

"Naw, you know it ain't like that. I just—"

"Who's this?" Country asked Rob, looking me up and down with shifty eyes.

I walked over to him. “How rude of me,” I said, extending my hand. “I’m Mike.”

That was how I found out that Country was the rude S.O.B. He refused to acknowledge my presence. He just turned his back and took a hit from the pipe. I didn’t get upset. I just smiled and shrugged my shoulders. “So you gonna give me that ride or what?” I asked Rob.

Drooling for the pipe, he answered meekly, “Give me like a half-hour.”

Country cut in, “Do me a favor and have that clown wait outside. All this talking is fucking up my high.”

Again I stepped in front of him and offered a friendly handshake. “Boss, my fault. I didn’t mean to interrupt y’all.”

Once more he turned his back to me, taking another hit. I turned away grinning at the fool. But a couple of steps later I froze. A feeling of vengeance came over me again. I whirled around, drew my gun and charged in on him, and pressed the weapon firmly against his head. He was so stunned he didn’t move. I jerked the crack-pipe out of his hand. The girl screamed and ducked under the table. I commanded Country to take off his clothes. “Strip!” I shouted.

“What?”

I didn’t repeat myself or hesitate. I just cocked back the gun’s safety and shot him once in the left leg. He crashed to the floor squealing in agony, “I’m sorry, man! I’m sorry!”

Casually, I bent down toward the girl under the table and trained the gun on her. “Uh, uh, baby girl, no hiding. Help your man get more comfortable.”

The girl slowly crawled out and started to remove Country’s clothes.

“Come on, Mike. Was that really necessary?” Rob pleaded.

"Yes, it was. They didn't want to share." I took a seat at the table, laid my gun in front of me and smoked the rest of their crack, while they watched me and couldn't do a damn thing about it. A few seconds later and I was in cocaine ecstasy. Some things you don't forget. I remember standing up and doing a little salsa dance towards the door. "Let's get the show on the road," I told Rob, then walked out.

After Rob drove me to Bridgeport and I collected my money from June-Bug, which wasn't easy, I went on a two-week crack-cocaine, binging-robbing spree. Finally, at about 2 a.m. one morning, I stumbled through the door at Grams', filthy and incoherent. This was the lowest point in my life. I was so far gone, so quickly that I was clearly going to be dead in a matter of days if something didn't change.

But I was hungry. I hadn't eaten in days, so I went into the kitchen and ransacked the refrigerator. Grams walked in unexpectedly as I was making a few ham-and-cheese sandwiches.

"What's this?" she asked, opening her palm showing me a used crack-pipe.

"That's not mine," I replied, and plunged back into the refrigerator. I took out a carton of orange juice and started to drink from the carton.

"The hell it's not! I was washing clothes, so I decided to wash yours and I found it in your bag!"

"Grams, I was holding it for somebody."

"In my house?"

My mind was in a fog. I snubbed her and went back to attacking the refrigerator, and finished making a couple of sandwiches. Grams grabbed a pot from the sink and threw it at me. I wasn't expecting that. I ducked and the pot hit the wall.

"Get out of my house!" she yelled. I left the kitchen and headed into the living room. She trailed me. "You better find Jesus and find him fast."

"Grams, where I'm going God's not coming," I replied, stuffing my clothes into a trash bag.

"God is everywhere. You just have to be willing to look for him."

* * *

I still remember her words as if I'd heard them yesterday. At the time, though, I didn't want to hear any preaching. I simply walked out the door. After leaving Grams' house I ended up on the porch of the off-campus apartment belonging to my college brother F-Troop. I knocked on the door.

Wayne, tired as hell, answered. "Mike, what's going on?"

"I need a place to stay."

"Get in here."

His apartment—a wide, one-level loft—was cluttered. My brothers were studious, heavily into their books, but they had little time to clean up after themselves. In the four months that I lived with Ted, Tre, Wayne, Eric and Mac, they somehow got me back on course. I quit drugs cold turkey. I'm talking no rehabilitation facilities or programs! Just being around positive and God-fearing friends proved a success. I followed them everywhere they went—like a lost puppy. When one of the guys went to work, I rose up and escorted him to work. When they went to the library, I went with them to read books on psychology. We did everything together. I hated exercising, but one of the rules for living in the house was waking up at 5 a.m. and jogging for a mile. Drugs, cigarettes and alcohol were prohibited in the house, and church was a big part of their lives, Mac being the most religious. I wasn't ready to start going to church either, but I had no choice. Every Sunday we'd go off to morning mass.

The day before I was to turn myself in we were playing our usual Friday night basketball game at Goffee Street Park, except this was a seven-series championship game. I'll never forget that night, one of the clearest, most beautiful Indian summer nights ever. The kind of night you didn't want to end, just capture its warm breeze in a bottle. In the middle of Game 3, I limped off the court.

"Come on, Mike, you can't be tired already? It's only Game 3," Ted laughed. "Wayne weighs a hundred pounds more than you and he's still standing," he said. Unsmiling, Wayne picked up the ball and playfully threw it at Ted.

"There's no sitting down. Get back in the game, Mike!" Tre chimed in. I waved my hand at him to say I was throwing in the towel, and plumped down on the bench.

"Take five, fellas," Mac announced, and joined me on the bench. "What's wrong, dog?"

"I'm not ready to leave you guys tomorrow."

"Let me explain something to you: God's not gonna put you in a situation he feels you can't handle."

"*God*," I sighed. "Please, don't start preaching to me."

"No—I'm not gonna preach. But you need to hear this. Think about the story of Job. Job was a very rich man, a faithful servant of God who was persecuted by the Devil, to the point of nearly losing his life. Everything was taken from Job—his health, his riches, his family. People told him to turn his back on God so he'd get his life back. But Job refused, and because of that God rewarded him twofold. Mike, you're Job. Now is the time for you to put your trust and faith in God."

Mac reached into his pocket and removed a gold chain with a small cross dangling on the end of it.

"You may not believe now, but get ready to witness a miracle," Mac said, placing the cross around my neck. "Now come on, we have a game to win and you have greatness to achieve."

I studied the cross for a moment, wiped the sweat from my forehead, and ran back on the court.

* * *

September 18, 1988 was the day I entered Cheshire Prison, a maximum level-five correctional facility. This is where the hardened criminals, rapist and coldblooded killers went. Now, I was tough but I was no heartless murderer. I was petrified. I knew I had to make friends fast.

There were five cellblocks, "A" through "F". I was placed in cell block "C" with 500 other prisoners. Three guards—one in the back, another in the middle and a third at the front of the line—took me and ten other incoming inmates down C-block's far-reaching corridor. We were dressed in our gray jump suits and shackled by our waists, ankles and wrist. I held my trash bag of pairs of jeans, T-shirts, socks, sneakers and the bible that Mac offered me. As we made our way past the cells, some convicts whistled, spitting at us and shouting profanities from their cells.

Finally, we stopped in the middle of the block. "Open the cells!" the guard in front radioed on his CB. Immediately, eleven heavy-metal doors slid open simultaneously in a thunderous BOOM. One by one, the guards released us from our chains and we stepped into our cells. I was the only inmate with no cellmate, and believe me, I wasn't disappointed. I set my bag down on the bottom bunk. My cell door automatically slammed shut. That was when I began to feel claustrophobic, hyperventilating as I looked around the diminutive space. The cell was so tiny I could touch the ceiling without stretching, and if I spread my arms out I could touch the walls. There was a bunk bed, a crusty commode and a sink that looked like it hadn't been cleaned in a decade or two.

I've never been to prison for any long period of time, much less a maximum-level facility. The first time I went behind bars was for a beating and shooting; I never got caught for all the other, small-time crimes. So, I lay on my bunk, my feet hanging off the edge and rubbing against the commode. God was putting me through this and I hated him for it! I blamed everyone else but myself: from the cat to Gary Parker, my parents, and every white person on the planet. Not once did I take responsibility for my own actions; my manhood wouldn't allow it. I managed to close my eyes for a moment, thinking of when I was a boy. How I loved baseball then! I imagined myself back on the field. It was pure, innocent happiness...

I heard loud moans and grunts nearby. Two men were having sex, and it made me cringe. I gripped the cross that hung on my neck and began to pray. I prayed to God as I had never done before, and it came straight from my heart this time. I didn't ask him to grant me miraculous freedom from this place but to help me endure it. Still, I wasn't sure I could trust him. I needed him to show me some kind of sign.

The first month was rough. I had severe stomach aches, and terrible nightmares about guards entering my cell while I slept and dragging me out of my bunk and leaving me in the corridors. There, rapacious prisoners awaited me, and I was passed to everyone on the block, before being thrown to a massive circle of merciless inmates, who proceeded to beat me senseless.

One day, while I sat in the mess-hall eating breakfast, which consisted of thick and clumpy oatmeal, a six-foot-three,

300-some-odd-pound black guy approached me. He looked like a grizzly bear, but scarier. I squeezed my fork ready to poke him between the eyes. "What are you doing in here?" the giant asked.

I put on a tougher-than-nails look and replied, "None o' your business."

The giant dude smiled at me. "Relax. I'm your cousin—Lumpy, your father's nephew."

My heart jumped from my gut and then back into my chest. "You're Curtis' nephew?"

"No, I'm your father Leroy's nephew. You don't remember me because the last time your father brought you to Grandma's house you was a real little guy."

Lumpy's eyes fell on the dude sitting beside me. Leave your food and beat it, he told him. The guy hurried out of his chair. Lumpy took his place and began to finish off his grub before touching his own.

"Anyways, I ran into your father right before I got locked up. He told me you'd be dropping in and asked me to look out for you."

I hadn't really talked to my biological father in ten or eleven years, though I used to bump into him periodically, because he lived in the area where I hung out at as a teenager. I didn't think he cared. He never did anything for me—until now. But the funny thing about street life was that everyone's always ear-hustling. Just when you think no one knows what you're doing or no one's listening, they are. In the case of Lumpy, I used to hear about him but I never met him. I knew he commanded a lot of respect and instilled fear in the streets. From the looks of it, the same went for this place.

"*Listen up!*" Lumpy, rising to his feet and snatching me

out of my chair, yelled to everyone in the dining hall. "This is my little cousin. Anyone fucks with him, fucks with me!"

Mac had told me I'd witness a miracle, and for the first time in my life, I saw God's work. Silently, I praised him. I made up my mind that from this day forward I would trust in God no matter what.

- 7 -

"...knowing that he who raised the Lord Jesus shall raise us also by Jesus and bring us with you in his presence. For it is all for your sake, so that as grace extends to more and more people it may increase thanksgiving, to the glory of God. So we do not lose heart. Though our outer nature is wasting away, our inner nature is being renewed every day," I was reading aloud to myself from 2 Corinthians 4:14-16 as I lay on my bunk.

The cell door slid open. Slowly I inched my bible away from my eyes to see who it was. A medium height, husky white kid, I'd say 19 or 20 years old, walked in like he was used to this kind of stuff and owned the place. The cell shut behind him.

"Damn, I can't stand these C.O.s. They think they're tough," was how he introduced himself to me. "I ever catch one of them on the streets, I'd beat the shit out of them."

I recognized a loudmouth, one of those white boys who watched too many rap videos and now thought that, because he knew a few Ice-T songs, he was down. It was all an act. I cut my eyes from the chump and went on reading my bible.

"So what are you in here for?" my new cellmate asked. I didn't respond. "Yo, dog, you hear me talking to you?"

"If it be so, our God whom we serve is able to deliver us from the burning, fiery furnace, he will deliver us out of thine hand, O King," I read out loud in prayer.

"Oh, I see, you on that holy shit."

The more that white boy talked, the more he got under my skin. Though I started to believe in God, I hadn't quiet put on the New Man that, according to Ephesians, God had created in righteousness and true holiness. I still hated white people: they were responsible for all my own misfortunes.

* *

Finally, he struck a nerve. "Man, all that God shit will get you killed in here," he declared, peering out of the cell.

"What did you say?" I put my bible down and eased off my bed. I was furious.

"In here God don't exist. You better wrap that around you head. And you weren't very hospitable," the new roomy said with a laugh. "But I'll let it slide this time. I might not be as nice next time though."

I flew off the bed and grabbed the wannabe thug by his neck and slammed him up against the cell door, where I started to choke the life out of him. He turned blue and foamed from the mouth. "Don't ever threaten me or disrespect God's word," I hoarsely whispered to his face. A guard was heading down the hall so I released the loudmouth punk from my clutches. The dude fell to the floor struggling to regain his breath. I went to the sink and washed my face to calm down.

Weeks later, out of the blue, I uttered the very first calm

words to him since that incident. "I shot a white boy." We were both lying on our bunks, and I was reading my bible as usual when I came across Romans 12: 17: "Recompense no man evil for evil. Provide things honest in the sight of all men." Reading this part of the scripture, it finally dawned on me that I had no right to harbor hatred in my heart towards anyone—even those who wronged me.

"What?" my cellmate asked.

"You asked me what I was in here for and I'm telling you. I shot a white boy, and I used to hate white people."

"Listen man, I'm really sorry about that comment I made during our first run-in. I had no right to disrespect your—"

"So what's your name?"

"Anthony."

"I'm Mike. What you in for?"

"Conspiracy to sell and distribute cocaine. I'm facing 25 years."

I chuckled a bit, because Anthony looked like Andy Griffin but acted like he was the *baddest* gangster alive. I figured he came from a well-to-do family, with a mom and dad who were happily married and had great careers, and a dog named Skip.

"So where you from?"

"Nagatuck, but I'm down with Bridgeport," Anthony said, throwing up a ridiculous gang sign with his fingers.

I laughed because Nagatuck was as clean and peachy as Middle America and apple pie. I never liked kids that had it all but were willing to throw their lives away either to prove something to their "friends" or to spite their parents, and Anthony was that kind of guy.

"Not much to do in Nagatuck, huh?"

"Hell no! Ain't shit to do in Nagatuck. That's why I broke

the fuck out of there. My parents are both doctors and they wanted me to study medicine, but I'm not with that. I'm a hustler. Besides, my mom and pops are bigoted assholes and hated the fact that I hung around black people."

"Guess you showed them, huh?" I said sarcastically.

"Man, I don't give a damn what they think. I was making money and I don't need them!"

"I wish I could say I don't need my parents."

"So who are you rolling with in here?"

"God."

"You're not afraid of gettin' hurt if you're not affiliated?"

"Not at all," I answered, and turned the page in my bible until I got to Jeremiah 1:8. "'Do not be afraid of their faces for I am with thee to deliver thee' is the utterance of the Lord. Do you know what that means?"

"No."

"It means that God is with you always if you open up your heart and accept him as your savior."

"*Lights out!*" shouted one of the guards down the hall. Seconds later everything went black, but that didn't stop me from studying my bible. I got out of bed, just as I had every night when the lights went out, sat down on the floor and rested my back against the cell bars to catch the moon's glare. I was determined. Nothing was going to stop me from learning about God and establishing a personal relationship with Him. I kept reading.

The next morning I went to the showers and washed up for church. We had church on Sundays. Pastor Williams, of the Third Street Baptist Ministries—a short, bony black man in his mid-fifties—was our visiting minister. He spoke with tremendous passion. His ministry hit close to home, because his son was murdered during incarceration. As I stood under the steamy water, the peaceful state of my mind was ruptured. Three Hispanic guys, tattoos all over their bodies, came in with a look on their face like they were looking for trouble. They glanced at me but walked right past because, although Lumpy had been shipped to another prison, they knew I was his cousin.

"There's our bitch," I heard one of them say with a heavy and gruff Puerto Rican accent. A slim, effeminate white boy was showering only a few feet away from me. I closed my eyes and began to laver up. They positioned themselves around him. Soap on my face, I opened my eyes just a bit. The three Hispanics cornered their mouse-like prey and started to kiss and rub their hands all over his body.

"That ass is looking *good* today, baby," one of them lustfully oozed.

"Come on, guys, don't do this. I still haven't healed from the last time," the white guy begged in a tense, high-pitched voice. The three kept on manhandling him.

I was used to fights breaking out in the showers; walking past a cell, I'd seen men having sex and heard them raping each other. But this was the first time I witnessed someone being raped. It was revolting. I quickly rinsed the soap off and hurried out of the showers.

After the church service, I entered my cell singing, "Just a closer walk with thee, granted Jesus is my plea. I'll be satisfied, as long as I walk close with thee."

With a far-off gaze, Anthony was standing at the window watching some inmates in the jail yard. He didn't seem like the chatterbox I'd come to tolerate. His hands fiddled and twitched from either pocket. Then, he turned to me with a grim look on his face.

While doing my pushups, I asked him, “Everything all right?”

“They gave me 25 years. Mike, I can’t do twenty-five. What am I gonna do?”

“You’re not gonna give up, that’s what you’re *not* gonna do,” I answered between pushups.

As soon as I finished the last one, Anthony stood before me holding a sharp blade, which he had broken from a shaving razor, and pointed it at his jugular.

“I’m just some rich white kid whose parents gave him everything. I’m not built for jail, Mike.” Illusions fall hard sometimes.

I hesitated. The last thing I wanted was to make a move that would cause him to act irrational. I lay on the floor to catch my breath for a few moments. “You are a son of God and he loves you. Don’t do this,” I consoled him. Slowly I rose to my feet. “‘Do not be afraid of their faces, for I am with thee to deliver thee’ is the utterance of the Lord.”

Anthony smiled. “You’re a good dude, Mike. Keep your head up.” Emotionless, he sliced himself across the neck.

“*C.O.*,” I screamed at the top of my lungs.

Anthony collapsed, blood gushing from his neck. I rocketed to my bunk, ripped the sheet off and cradled him in my arms. With all my strength, I pressed the sheet against his neck to stop the bleeding.

“*C.O.! C.O! We need an ambulance*,” I screamed over and over again.

A corrections officer bolted to my cell and saw Anthony losing a great deal of blood. “Open cell 14 and get an ambulance *now*!” he hollered.

* * *

In prison I was allowed contact visits. One day my mother came to see me, a full thirteen months after I went in. I guess her conscience was beginning to eat at her. Pop had never visited me once. There was nothing I could do about that. He was a stubborn, tough-love kind of a man. As she and I sat in a visiting hall of twelve rows of long tables and uncomfortable wood chairs, eight guards—two by the exit signs in the corners—patrolled.

"So how are you doing in here?" Mom somberly asked.

"I'm holding up. I'm in God's hands. I've been praying for a job, but there hasn't been any available. Anyways, how's Pop?"

"He's good. An' how's the food?"

"Mom, I know Pop's not my real father, but what does he have against me?"

"Why would you *say* that?"

"My whole life he's never supported me."

"Your father supports you."

"Ma, stop covering up for him! When I was young playing baseball, he never came to my games. This is the first time you've come to see me since I been here, and Pop doesn't show up. That says it all."

As I was saying this, I spotted a small-framed, older white woman in her early 50s with heavy bags under her eyes and balding brunette hair. She was talking to a guard and pointing at me. That made me nervous, and I kept my eye on her.

The lady walked over to me. "Excuse me. I'm sorry to interrupt you, but are you Michael Daluz?"

"Yes, I am."

"Hi, my name's Mrs. Bendino, Anthony's mother."

I stood up and shook her hand. "Nice to meet you, Mrs. Bendino. I'm sorry about Anthony, how is he?"

"He's coming along. He was transferred to Connecticut mental health about two months ago."

"He'll be okay."

"I just want to thank you for saving my son."

"No thanks necessary."

Silence.

"Mrs. Bendino, this is my mother—Mrs. Texeria."

They shook hands. "You have a wonderful son," she told my mom. "You're very lucky."

"Thank you."

"Well, I should be going. May God bless you," Mrs. Bendino said to me.

"He already has," I replied.

- 8 -

I went to speak with the warden about getting a job and was told there was none. I returned to my cell frustrated, at my wit's end. To my utter surprise, a dozen letters were piled up on my bed. I sat down on my bunk and started to go through them. They were from people from all over the state—both black and white, but more from white folks. They all supported me over the shooting and told me they loved me. It was hard to believe. The more I read the more inspired I became.

One letter in particular really touched me. It was from a white woman who lived in a part of the state where gun violence—or any type of crime, for that matter—was virtually unheard of. "Dear Michael," she wrote me:

> My name is Elizabeth Smart. I am a white woman from Avon Connecticut. I have read your story in the papers and I just want you to know that I think what happened to you is repulsive. And as a Christian, I love you and I am praying for you. God is going to see you through

this and every experience in your life will only make you stronger.

First John 4:8 says: Beloved ones, let us continue loving one another because love is from God and everyone who loves has been born from God and gains the knowledge of God. He that does not know love has not come to know God, because God is love.

I was moved by Mrs. Smart's letter and all the letters of encouragement that poured in. They helped me realize that we are all God's creatures. We're imperfect, we err, but everyone is the same. They also helped me to see that God's love is far greater than the Devil's cunning and despairing hatred. I stayed up all night writing back to my Christian brothers and sisters, on the cusp of a fantastic healing process.

The next morning the cell doors opened. A guard shouted, *Breakfast!* I stepped outside. The hallways looked like lunch-hour traffic in New York City much as it always had. This time, though, a guard stopped and told me to report to the Warden's office. Though I hadn't done anything wrong, I was a bit worried about what the warden might say to me. Still, I prayed and hoped against hope that he may surprise me with something like, *Daluz you can leave right now*. Fat chance!

Knock, knock.

"Come in," Warden Freedmont said.

I walked into a dull, uninviting office. Freedmont's office was almost as bad as my cell. "Have a seat, Daluz," he instructed. I sat down on this hard-as-steel chair, my heart beating like a drum. "I know you've been requesting work. I have a job for you. Thanks to your heroism, it's a job cleaning the inside and outside of my office three days a week."

I was speechless. I'd been praying incessantly for any kind of job at all and I just landed the best job of all! Not only that, but now I could work outside too! What a blessing. *Hallelujah!*

"You can start tomorrow at 7 a.m. sharp," Freedmont he went on.

"You won't be disappointed, sir. Thank you, thank you so much."

When I left his office, I fell on my knees and started to pray right there in the middle of the corridor. I didn't care that everyone was staring at me. I was beginning to fathom the message that God was giving me: There is nothing he can't do for you.

* * *

When I first stepped out the front door leading from the Warden's office directly on to the street, during work, I breathed deeply. I had to take in the city air. It was exhilarating. It was as if I had stepped out in the world for the first time in my life. I sat on the steps for a while. I was so close to the curb I could almost touch the passersby. I watched the cars and buses roll by, observing all the faces. My eyes fell briefly on a gorgeous-looking woman jogger. She had long legs and wore tight shorts and a tank top. I waved. She smiled and winked at me. I was really taken by her beauty.

Out of the blue, the sound of ragged wheels squeaking down the block and of clanging bottles and cans reached my ears. Someone was loudly whistling a familiar tune: "*I want you to walk, walk with me. Yes, I want you to walk, walk with me*," the lyrics echoed in my head.

I bounced to my feet looking this way and that to see where the noise was coming from. Then, there he was, the same old scummy drifter I had seen shortly before going to prison stood on the opposite side of the street. He dug through his shopping cart and took out a cardboard sign that read: TRUST IN THE LORD WITH ALL YOUR HEART AND DO NOT LEAN UPON YOUR OWN UNDERSTANDING. IN ALL YOUR WAYS TAKE NOTICE OF HIM AND HE WILL MAKE YOUR PATH STRAIGHT.

After that he trundled down the street.

I flew down the stairs after him. "Hey! Hey, you!" I shouted.

The Warden flung open his screen door. "*Daluz,* get back here!" he ordered.

I froze in my tracks. I walked backwards onto the porch. By then the drifter had vanished. I looked in every direction hoping for his return.

"Let's go, Daluz!"

I went back into the building feeling more confident than ever about my faith, and *very* eager to complete my remaining time. I've since understood that it was another vision from God.

* * *

I was released from prison on March 8, 1990, and sent to live at the *Better Living Halfway House*, a faith-based housing facility in New Haven geared to drug addicts and ex-cons. That meant that Godly principles formed the foundation of the house. I sat in the director's cluttered office-bedroom. He called himself Mr. V.

"One, everyone must be in bed by 8 p.m., if you're not working," he instructed me on arrival. "Two, you're not permitted to leave the building or look for a job for the first thirty-five days. Three, you must have employment after thirty days of job hunting, or I will find one for you. And four, you must attend three counseling groups a day and two NA meetings per week." After explaining the rules of the house to me, he asked me if I had any questions.

"No, sir. I thank you for the opportunity."

"I'm not gonna be easy on you, Daluz."

"No problem. I'm not used to things being easy on me," I answered.

* * *

"Hello, how are you? My name's Michael Daluz. I'm interested in finding work," I told the receptionist.

I'd been at the halfway house for thirty-five days. This was the first day I was allowed to leave the house and look for a job. I was determined to find work. I was ready to move on with my life and become a productive citizen again, no matter what it took. There I was—cuddling a newspaper under my armpit in front of the receptionist's desk at the Elm City Temp agency, and dressed *very* casually. Slacks, button-down shirt, tie and a cheap pair of sneakers. With my $40 weekly allowance, I had no money to buy a pair of shoes.

"Do you have a criminal record?" the receptionist asked in a demeanor that screamed attitude. I didn't want to tell her I had just been released from prison, but I had no choice. I knew they'd do a thorough background check. It was humiliating, because the place was packed with potential new hirees. I felt all eyes upon me.

I leaned against her window and whispered, "Yes. I was just released from prison."

"Well, we don't hire anyone with a criminal background."

"Thank you," I answered with a faint smile and walked out. Next...

At the Drake Lumber Warehouse, I had to yell over loud machines to be heard. "*I've done warehouse work before…I was a forklift driver…for about a year while in college.*" The manager closely reviewed my application, as we stood in the middle of the busy shop. "*I didn't mention this on the application, but I also worked for my neighbor's machine shop during high school.*"

The manager showed me around the place, introducing me to employees. I figured, wham, I'm gonna get this job! But then he came across the question on the application where you're asked about any criminal record.

"Says here that you have a felony. What were you in prison for?"

"Attempted murder, in 1987."

"Thank you for your interest. I'll keep your application on file," he promptly informed me.

I must have put in at least twenty applications a week, and this was the last day for me to find a job. Back at the halfway house I felt hopeless. I climbed the stairway up to my room completely despondent and just dropped on my bed. The rooms were small. Ours had a cement floor, an old-fashion radiator, a tight window, very uncomfortable beds, a tiny black-and-white television set stacked on a couple of crates, and a tattered dresser. Every piece of furniture in the house was a hand-me-down donated by the Salvation Army. There were about sixty of us in the house. Most stayed to themselves.

Frank Ellise, a fellow resident, was sitting on the other bed playing gin with another guy. "So how did the job hunt go today, Mike?"

"Not good. I can't find anything."

"Well, that punk, V, will assign you a job. Good luck, 'cause it'll probably be a crappy gig."

"Hey, a gig's a gig," I answered.

"Yeah, well, look out for that character V," warned the man Frank was playing cards with. "I don't trust him."

"I don't trust anyone except God."

Just then, one of the workers popped his head through at the door and said, "Hey, Mike, you got a phone call downstairs."

Lackadaisically, I rose up asking who it was. "Some chick name Terry," he said.

A rush jolted my body. I had bumped into her one fine day on the bus and given her the phone number to my halfway house. I had waited almost two weeks for her to call me. She wasn't really my type, physically speaking. I was used to girls that looked like models, Danielle being a prime example. Terry wore glasses and was very plain-looking, but she had tons of personality and intelligence. That was what attracted me to her the most. That said, she still had the sexiest and longest pair of legs I'd ever laid eyes on. Besides, after being locked up for eighteen months, I had a chance to be close to a woman.

I shot off the bed and practically flew down the stairs. "Hello!" I spoke into the receiver like a dog in heat.

"Hi, Michael. It's Terry, how are you?

"I know who this is. It took you long enough to call me, girl," I said playfully.

"Yeah, I was pretty busy with work and all."

"A renaissance woman—I like that."

She giggled. "So who is Michael?" she said.

"What do you mean?"

"Well. Tell me about yourself."

I paused. I really didn't want her to judge me like everyone else: an ex-con without a pot to piss in or a window to throw it out of. Somehow, I had to bite the bullet. To be honest, all I wanted from Terry was sex. Nothing more, nothing less.

"Well, Michael is a U.S. Army Veteran," I explained, "a once-upon-a-time college student and an ex-convict. You can hang up now. I'd understand if you didn't want to talk to me anymore."

"Listen, you don't have to explain. Everyone makes mistakes. You've paid your debt to society and you deserve a second chance."

"So...can we go out for a cup of coffee or lunch sometime? I'm a free man on the weekends."

She laughed. "You're funny. I like a man with a sense of humor. But sure, Michael, we can go out sometime."

I was enjoying the conversation. "How's this weekend?"

"That sounds good."

I was unimaginably overjoyed at the prospect of seeing her this weekend. I had a feeling I may get lucky putting on the old Mike charm, not that I thought she was easy. At this point in my life I was learning about God, but a lot of my bad habits lingered on inside me, such as my womanizing. I was about to turn up the heat with Terry over the phone, when Mr. V. tapped me on my shoulder. "Daluz, I need to talk to you—in my office, *now*."

I sighed. "Okay, so I'll see you this weekend, Ms. Terry."

I hung up and followed Mr. V. into his office.

"I know you've been working hard at finding a job, but you know the rules. It's been thirty days and you haven't reported anything to me yet. I got two job offers for you. One is at an apartment building sitting at a desk signing people in and out. The job pays eight-fifty an hour. The other job pays $4.75 an hour, but I feel it builds character." He slid out his desk drawer, reached in and tossed a *Roy Roger's* hat on his desk. "You can start tomorrow at 5:30 a.m."

I stared at the hat, as if the ground had just caved in from under my feet.

"Try your new hat on," he poked fun. I snatched the hat off of his desk and stormed away. "I told you I wasn't gonna be easy on you!" he said.

- 9 -

For the next five months, my alarm clock went off every day at 3:30 in the morning. *Ri-i-i-i-ng!* I got up to say my prayers, shower, shave and eat breakfast, which consisted of a slice of toast, a bowl of oatmeal and a grape fruit. I left the house at 4:15 and walked to Roy Rogers. That was a seven-mile hike, because buses didn't start running until 5:20 a.m. It was definitely a testament to my manhood and my faith. Some days brought pouring rain, others snow and cold so raw that by the time I got to work the tips of my socks were occasionally stained with blood. The morning trip exhausted and often sickened me. One pair of sneakers began to turn over with small holes. But I didn't complain. I knew this struggle was bringing me a step closer to God. I had decided to be the best *Roy Roger* employee that I could be.

Kate, a high-strung white woman, was my supervisor. She came into the men's room once as I was scrubbing the decay off of the toilets. "Michael, as soon as you're done in here, I need you to take out the garbage...and sweep the parking lot. It looks a mess."

"Yes ma'am."

"Thanks, Mike, that's why you're my best employee," she assured me. She was about to leave the bathroom then paused and turned to me, "How do you do it?"

"Do what?"

"Come in here so happy and put up with this shitty job?"

"God and God only."

She smiled at me. "Well, God bless you."

"Thanks, Kate."

When I finished cleaning the bathroom, I went outside to straighten up the parking lot, just as Kate had asked me. But it was hard rain out there and I got drenched. I had to lug three heavy bags of trash to the dumpster without the bags busting. Along the way, one hole in my sneakers grew bigger and exposed a couple of my toes. In the tussle, the garbage bags burst, spilling debris all over. I stood dumbfounded, surrounded by garbage and my feet sopped. I could feel myself losing my cool.

But my first reflex was to fold my hands and say a prayer. Jail had been a humbling experience. It taught me to be grateful for every day for being alive. It taught me to stop complaining. You see, the truth is that no one respects a complainer. People respect those who accept the challenge and are ready to fight. More importantly, I had developed a true friendship with God. It's a bit like when you and your girl are true friends. I'm not talking about a sexual partnership where y'all pay the bills together. I'm talking about true friendship, where you tell her everything. And when you're having the worst day ever, you call her up. That's what I began to have with God, and it's beautiful.

Drenched and tired as hell, I came home whistling a song of joy. *Just a closer walk with thee*—I sang. I sprinted up the steps of the halfway house and down the hall to Mr. V's office. *Whap, whap!*

"Come in," Mr. V shouted above the din of the television blaring behind the door. I entered and shut the door behind me. Mr. V was relaxing, his feet on the desk, watching a game between the Boston Celtics and the Chicago Bulls. *From half-court, Jordon shoots and he scores! The Bulls have won again!*" screamed the sports commentator. *Bird and his Celtics can't stop Jordon!*"

"What was that!" Mr. V roared at the television set. His big eyes bulging out of his head, he grabbed the remote off his desk and turned the set off. He looked kind of like a black exploitation cartoon from the early 1950s. One look at me and he exclaimed, "Man, someone had a rough day."

"No, my day was wonderful. Look, can I get an advance on my check this week? I need new sneakers...my toes are playing peek-a-boo."

Mr. V. looked at my sneakers and chuckled. He opened his desk drawer and flung a roll of duct tape at me.

I caught it. "What's this?"

"Your advance for a new pair of sneakers."

"What am I supposed to do with this?"

"Figure it out."

"Man, I need new shoes! I walk to work every morning and I don't have a decent pair of shoes!"

"Daluz, I told you I wasn't gonna be easy on you. This is your test. Your journey. We all have a test and a journey. Some people's test and journey is harder than others. You're not like the rest of these guys in here. You're smart. You're driven. We're brothers embodied by Christ and you won't break.

When you're preparing your place with the heavenly father, you will suffer."

"Haven't I done enough suffering?"

"This is just the beginning, young blood. The Devil's coming for you more than you know," he said, and chuckled some more. "Get ready."

"I'm trying."

"Daluz, keep running. Never stop running! The moment you stop running the Devil will catch you. Stay in prayer."

After talking to him, I went into the bathroom and took my shower. As the hot water relaxed my body, I broke down and cried like a baby for the first in my life. I had cried when I was a child, but never as a man. Not even when I got my head beat in. Never shed a tear. I was too strong and prideful for that. But everything was now weighing down on me, and I wasn't sure if I could handle it anymore. Then, I remembered Mac's words about God not piling up more on you that you can't handle.

I dried off, got dressed and then sat on the edge of the tub to wrap duck tape around my left foot sneaker. If this was how it had to be right now, so be it. I was on a journey. I was preparing my place with my heavenly father. Nothing else mattered.

* * *

When I was laid off that job, I went to see my tax accountant at the Liberty Tax office. "Well, Mr. Daluz, looks like you'll be getting back $312.56," he announced.

"May I see that?"

"Absolutely," handing me the pay stubs he'd calculated.

I scratched my head in confusion because I couldn't

understand how I could have worked so many hours and only received only $312 in returns. "I don't get it."

"Well, the government comes for the poor first and taxes low-income Americans the most. You being in that low-income bracket—it's a shame."

"Yeah, it is."

He gazed down at my sneakers. "I don't mean to get in your business, but are you currently employed?"

"No, I'm not. I got laid off last week."

"Well, we have positions open for the tax season. It doesn't pay much but it's an easy job. Are you interested?"

"Work is work in my book."

"I'll get you some paperwork to fill out. Can you start tomorrow?"

"I sure can."

The next morning I stood in bone-chilling weather dressed in a Lady Liberty costume and holding a sign advertising LIBERTY TAX SERVICES. I had to wave to the motorists driving by. Not exactly what I was expecting, I guess, but I needed "to build character." God wasn't through with me yet, I thought to myself.

* * *

"So what was it like being in the army?" Terry asked, while we lounged at a cozy coffee shop on a Saturday afternoon, as though she were conducting an interview. She was dressed very tomboyish, like a woman who'd just rolled out of bed with her hair in a pony-tail, wearing a baseball cap and a jogging suit. She'd been reading a book titled *Ten Reasons Men Are Afraid Of Commitment*.

"The army was hard at first, because I was hardheaded. I had issues with authority."

"And why's that?"

"It started when I was fifteen. I was a good kid, but I had problems with my mom and stepdad—him especially. I felt left out in my family, which led me to get involved with the wrong crowd. Anyways, my mom made me go into the army thinking it might help me. In a way it did."

"Hmm...I see."

I must admit, I was turned on. She wasn't like the other females I'd known; they who went out of their way to impress me. For the first time, I felt a little unsure of myself in the presence of a woman—somewhat like the once-upon-a-time man. Maybe my personal hardships made me feel this way. But Terry was still not my type.

"You know, you've been reading that book since I sat down," I said.

"What can I say? It's a good book."

"I'm sure it is. But you haven't made eye contact with me at all."

"I'm sorry," she said, still refusing to look at me.

I shrugged it off with a slight laugh and decided to turn on the ole Mike Daluz charm. I reached over and gently touched her chin and lifted her head. "The shape of your eyes is beautiful." She cracked a smile. "Is that a smile I see trying to break through?"

I carefully removed her glasses and set them on the table. She tried to grab them back, but I blocked her hand and continued to caress her face. I'm not proud to claim this now, but I knew then that Terry had fallen under my spell.

"So tell me, who's Terry?" I said.

When I carried her into her bedroom that night, our lips were locked like a combination to a safe. I laid her on the bed and began to undress her, kissing her all over. She moaned and melted in my hands. I was so excited the furthest thing from my mind was using protection. It was one of the biggest mistakes of my life. But we had mind-blowing sex for hours on end.

After leaving Terry's apartment, I went back to the halfway house, where I headed towards the bathroom for a shower, when Mr. V stopped me. "Hey, Daluz," he shouted from behind and approached me from down the hall. I stopped.

Placing his arm around me the way a father would his son, he said, "Mike, you've been one of the best clients I've ever had. You're a hard worker, you stay out of trouble, and you put up with me. As you know, your time is almost up here and I'd like to see you go with a job."

"I appreciate that, sir."

"A construction company called — Brick-By-Brick Construction. They're looking to hire a guy from my program. The job pays seventeen bucks an hour. You start tomorrow 8 a.m., on the dot."

I was elated. "Thank you, sir." I embraced him with all my might. "Thank you, God!"

- 10 -

By the spring of 1991, I had worked at Brick-By-Brick construction for over three months, and Terry was six months pregnant. Besides that last development, my life had really begun to turn around. I was feeling good about myself. I had both my own apartment—small, but it was mine—and a job that I finally enjoyed.

I worked eight hours a day, five days a week in a seven-story building's cold, dilapidated basement that was half the size of a football field. All the floors in the building had been ripped up. Looking up from the basement, you could see straight to the top level. My area was marked Boilers 1, 2 and 3. Thirty- to forty-strong, we were divided into two crews. The blue crew was the night workers; their job was to knock out the bricks along the walls of each floor. The red crew, the day workers, had to dispose of the bricks that fell into the basement. I was with the latter.

From day one on the job, the site's supervisor assured us all that we were working under safe conditions. One day, as my crew was filling their barrows with bricks from a pile that seemed mountain-high, an avalanche of bricks collapsed from the fifth floor into the basement. The co-workers and I scattered in a flash before anyone was injured.

As the dust settled, Hunt, our foreman, cried out, "Is everyone ok?"

Yeah, we all replied.

"Everyone, take ten while I inform the site supervisor." We were glad to be taking time off to cool our heels, because those bricks got pretty heavy after a while. Hunt radioed the site supervisor, who was working in Boiler 3. "Leo, come in! Leo, come in!"

"*Yeah?*"

"We just had an avalanche of bricks fall from the fifth floor into boiler one! We probably need to call it a day, or at least check all floors to make sure it's safe to continue working."

"*Was anybody hurt?*"

"No."

"*Then have your men get back to work.*"

"Copy." Hunt looked at us. "Break's over, back to work."

The crew and I complained, because we didn't feel safe. Jerry Garcia stood up and told him, "Sir, it's not safe under there, and we're not working until they secure the area above us." Me and the other guys agreed with him.

Hunt again radioed the supervisor. "Come in, Leo."

"*Yeah.*"

"My men are complaining that it's not safe. They're refusing to work."

"*You tell them to get back to work or they're fired.*"

"Copy." Hunt let out a heavy sigh and turned to us. "Everyone, back to work or you're out of a job."

Some of the men wasted no time; they just walked off. The

majority stayed, I being one of them. I didn't have a choice. I was going to have a daughter in less than three months and I needed the money. So, I put my gloves on and went back to work. I didn't talk much on the job, no one did, but I was cool with a guy named Ron McCormick, a baseball fanatic like me.

"Hey, did you catch the sco' to last night's game?" Ron asked me in his Boston drawl.

"Yeah, the Yankees won 4 to 1."

"Damn! I lost a hundred dalla's," he plaintively confessed.

"I told you there was no way the Yanks could...," I was telling him when, without warning, bricks came toppling on top of me.

When I woke up three days later, I was lying in a hospital bed with bandages wrapped around my head. I was wearing a neck brace and hooked up to a breathing machine. My friends, Mac, Eric, Wayne and Ted—Tre had been in California on business—were at my bedside. They were overjoyed when I woke up. We were at last reunited, as we hadn't seen each other since my prison time.

"Hallejulah!" Mac shouted, grabbing my hand.

"Welcome back, Mike," Eric said, and everyone clapped.

"How did you know what happened," I mumbled in pain.

"Well, I went to your mom's house and she told me. So I called the boys and here we are," Wayne explained. Then, I felt a gentle kiss on my forehead. It was my mother. My vision was blurry, but I could recognize her scent anywhere; she always smelled like apples and cinnamon. I didn't expect my stepfather to come, but I heard a voice say, "How are you, son?" Believe me, just knowing my stepfather was there and hearing him call me "son" remains one of my fondest memories.

I smiled. "Am I dead?"

"*No*, you're not *dead*, thank God," Pop said. There was a quiver in his voice, as though he wanted to cry.

Just then Doctor Katz walked in. "Can everyone excuse us? Except for Mr. and Mrs. Texeria."

"Mike, we'll be here, brother," Ted informed. He and the guys stepped outside.

"What's the problem, Doctor?" Pop asked. Long silence. "Would you just tell me what's wrong with my son," he pleaded.

"The X-rays show that Michael suffered tremendous damage to the brain, which greatly impairs his vision, and his spinal cord is also damaged. It's unclear at the moment if he'll ever function the same. I'm so sorry," he said and exited the room.

My mother cried her eyes out. I had never seen her so emotional or seen my parents so supportive. I wondered if someone was playing a trick on me. But it felt good. God sure has a way of changing people's hearts. This is not to say that my parents didn't love me before; they just had a funny way of showing it.

"I don't remember a thing," I said to them.

"Just relax, baby," my mother comforted me.

"You're lucky to be alive, son," Pop assured me.

"God has a plan for me."

He turned to my mom and asked, "Honey, would you leave us alone for a few minutes?"

"Sure. I'm gonna go down to the café and get something to eat—I haven't eaten all day," she said. She kissed me on the cheek and left the room. Pop went over to the window to look up at the starry sky, slowly rubbing his hands together. He began to massage his forehead. Whenever he did that, he had something to apologize for and was searching for words.

"Look, I'm sorry," he said.

"Sorry for what, Pop?"

"For making you feel unloved. It's just that my father was so tough on me, so I thought—"

"Pop, I understand."

There was a long moment of silence.

"Well, it's getting late. I'm gonna head home. Tell your mom I left."

"I will, Pop." He headed for the door, but before stepping out he paused and looked at me. With tears in his eyes, he confessed, "I love you, son."

"Love you too, Pop." Pop and I never became best of friends, as such, but we did find mutual respect and understanding.

Over the course of sixteen weeks, I underwent extensive physical therapy. I was able to walk and gained feeling on my left side. When I recovered enough, I was released from hospital. Though I was able to get around on my own, I wasn't the same. I had to walk with a cane for a long time; I suffered from chronic back spasms, headaches and horrific nightmares, which allowed me no more than two to three hours of sleep a night. And soon after my release, I was diagnosed with Post-traumatic Stress Disorder. I decided to sue Brick-By-Brick Construction for negligence.

On top of all that, I had a daughter I hadn't seen since she was born, on June 7, 1991, because Terry and I had become estranged. When I paid Terry a visit at her apartment, I didn't get a pleasant greeting. A strange woman opened the door, who I found out was her mom.

"Who are you?" she asked, gazing at me with suspicion.

"Who is it, Mom?" Terry yelled out from inside. I could hear my daughter crying in the background.

"It's that son of a bitch, Michael."

"Mom, can you take over and feed the baby?"

Her mother gave me the evil eye then walked away, saying, "Come on, baby, grandma got you."

Terry came to the door. "Well, well, look who decides to show up. You look like shit."

"Come on, please don't start. You know I had an accident on the job, I nearly died."

"Well, I wish you had."

"Whatever, can I see my daughter please?"

She stepped toward me into the hallway, shutting the entrance door behind her. "Can you see *your* daughter? She's not your daughter. She's *my* daughter!"

"Look Terry, I know you're still angry at me for telling you that I didn't want a relationship, but don't take it out on our daughter. I tried to be there for you during the pregnancy, but you didn't want my help. What was I supposed to do?"

Terry let out an insane laugh.

"You didn't want a relationship? You should've thought of that before you fucked me!" she said fiercely but in a low tone. "Since you didn't want a relationship, you don't need a relationship now with my baby."

"Terry, we had sex—*once*. Can I least know my daughter's name?"

"Her name's *fuck you*!" She slid back and slammed the door in my face. I began to feel my blood boil and those old violent feelings resurface. Somehow I was able to keep my cool, for my daughter's sake, but some old bad habits of mine were crawling under my skin—that itch, that urge to do away with an ugly reality. Basically I needed to get high. So I returned to a place I was familiar with, Rob's house. I used to get high with Rob. Only, I didn't know if he still lived there, or if he was even alive. I took a chance.

Some people never change. Rob was still doing the same

thing he was doing in 1987, except now he looked like the walking dead. "What's up, Rob, how are you?" I greeted him.

"Who are you?" he asked, foaming from the mouth like he was in the middle of getting blasted.

"It's Mike."

"Mike who?"

I was offended. "The only Mike that used to save your ass."

He finally responded, with a twitch. "Oh, Mike! Hey, hey, it's Mike!"

"Yeah, it's me."

"So what you doing around here?"

"Come on, man, you know what time it is?" I said, and stepped into his filthy apartment. The smell was nauseating. The place was an orgy drug fest. My base impulse told me I wanted to join them in their painless, zombie state. My mind and heart told me I shouldn't have come here in the first place.

I ended up standing in the corner watching in disbelief: I used to live almost like this. God had pulled me up from under those bricks and I was repaying him by spitting in his face and going back to this appalling life. Watching these people fight over money and drugs made me see his grand purpose for me, for the first time: I wanted to dedicate my life to helping people with drug addiction.

After fleeing Rob's apartment, I spent weeks researching drug rehabilitation centers across the state of Connecticut in hopes of finding a job. Everyone turned me down. They said I didn't have "work-related experience" or schooling. So I began thinking about going back to school. Then I stumbled on a place called, The Elm City Drug Counseling Center. It was owned by a black doctor named Thomas Gains, a graduate of

Yale University. I showed up at his office the next day prepared to do whatever it took to get a job.

Sitting at his desk eating a salad, Dr. Gains bluntly told me, "I can't hire you, I'm sorry. You don't have any background in this field."

"With all due respect, sir, I lived it. I know what these people are going through mentally, physically and emotionally."

"Living it helps but it's not enough. You need the educational aspect as well."

"Well, I'm in the process of going back to school to get my associate's degree."

Dr. Gains chuckled. "You're gonna need much more than an associate's, son. But I admire your motivation. Everything you've told me you've been through shows that you have strong will. Unfortunately, I still can't hire you."

"Thank you for your time, sir. Have a good day."

As I was walking out, he stopped me. "Wait. Have a seat."

I sat back down with my ears wide open. He stared at me wordlessly for a while. I felt a little uncomfortable and stared right back at him. "Do you believe in God?"

"Yes, I do."

He put down his fork and wiped his mouth with a napkin. He analyzed me visually for what seemed like an eternity. "I don't usually do this...I'm being totally unethical right now. But God is telling me that I should do it, so I'll tell you what—" Then the phone rang, and he excused himself. "Dr. Gains, how can I help you?" he answered.

I sat there gazing at all his academic degrees and the awards he'd won for community activism, and I thought: I want to experience what it's like to give back to society in such an inspiring way.

"Hey, listen, I'm in the middle of a meeting. I'll call you

back," he told the person on the other end. He hung up and turned to me. "As I was saying, it's gonna take you a little over two years to get your associate's. But if you abide by a few stipulations I'll put down, I will train you myself and you can start working for me while you're in school."

"I'm willing to do whatever it takes, sir. I just want to help people."

"Very well, then, you must get straight A's. I don't want to see anything less than that. You will need to join a black-counselor organization, attend conferences, read the autobiography of Malcolm X, and watch two movies: X and a documentary on Martin Luther King. Focus on how they spoke. After you start school you have a minimum of six months to fulfill this or the deal is off. I'm a very busy man and I don't have time for people who are not focused or serious."

"I understand. Thank you, sir." I shook his hand.

I wasted no time setting to work. I enrolled in school, got financial aid and began attending classes all in the span of a few weeks. I found a lot on my plate at once, of course. During my first two months in school I had five surgeries, three on my back and two on my eyes. I couldn't bend over or lift anything that was more than thirty pounds. I also suffered from acute migraines and double vision, and I had to wear a patch over my right eye. There were times when I had to be rushed to hospital from school after passing out. But one thing I could say about my days in military service: it taught me always to be prepared and to endure the physical pain. I endured every day I was fighting the pain. I wasn't about to look back. I was moving forward full force.

Despite the obstacles, I scored at the top of my class and uniformly turned in A-graded papers. I know for certain that God was with me the entire time.

* * *

"Hey, Terry, I apologize for calling at this hour, but I need to talk to my daughter. May I speak to her?"

"You got a nerve calling me. *Fuck off!*" She slammed the phone in my ear.

There was just no getting through to her. My daughter was almost a year old and I hadn't seen her once. I tried to reason with Terry; I'd been patient and hopeful she might come around and realize that a child needs its father too. But that phone call got me fed up. I decided to go to her house. It was a bad idea, but I really needed to see my daughter.

I got dressed and drove over. I rang the doorbell at one o'clock in the morning and waited to be buzzed into the building. Terry answered the intercom in an aggravated and sleepy voice. "Who *is* it?"

"Michael."

"What do you want?"

"I want to see my daughter."

"The only thing you're about to see is the inside of a jail cell if you don't leave me alone."

"You're not gonna threaten me with the police! I don't care if you call the police. Go ahead, call them!"

"Aren't you still on probation?" she seethed.

I calmed down. She had me.

"That's what I thought. So you have five seconds to leave this building."

"Fine. Can you at least tell me her name?"

"Goodbye, Michael."

I was so infuriated I punched a hole in the intercom panel before leaving the building.

- 11 -

On January 26, 1993, I entered Dr. Gain's office feeling proud of myself. I had fulfilled everything he had asked of me and more in two semesters. Now I was eager to learn as much as I could from him.

I dropped a thick booklet down on his desk. He glanced at it, then looked at me staidly. Skimming through it, he learned about my A-graded test papers and scholarship honor awards; about making it each semester to the university Dean's list, the national Dean's list and the presidential list. I remember that moment well. Without saying a word, he stood up and shook my hand.

I felt resurrected from the dead. I'd had a lot to prove to myself, and now I could attest that no matter how ferociously the Devil attacks you, God will always win!

"We start on Monday," Dr. Gains looked honestly pleased to announce. "Step one, you have to acquire a distaste for drugs and alcohol. Step two, you have to begin to see yourself as worthy of living. Step three, and the most important, is believing in God and his grand purpose for you. If you begin to apply all three of these steps in your everyday life, you will have a successful recovery."

It took me eight months to complete my training. I started working as a counselor in September 1993. Sitting in a circle with a group of addicts and alcoholics, I was in awe of having made it this far.

"All you have to do is believe," I assured the clients. "It may sound to you like a corny line from a Walt Disney movie, but it's true."

"That's easier said than done, Mike. You're not in our shoes," Troy Gibson retorted.

"I once was in your shoes, but I made a choice to change. 'Do I want to change?' is the question you have to ask yourself?"

"Yes, I do, but it's hard. Sometimes I want to say fuck it and disappear."

"Troy, where do you want to be in ten years?"

"I'm a mechanic, I want to own my own business and marry my girl. She left me because of my drug habit."

"Do you like boxing?"

"Yeah."

"Who's your favorite boxer?"

"Tyson. And don't judge him for losing the belt to that chump, Buster Douglas. It was a setup."

I laughed, dismissing his comment. "Tyson was good but Ali was the greatest," I replied.

"What? Mike, are you gonna sit there and tell me that Ali was better than Tyson."

"Absolutely."

"Man, you're crazy!" He and the other clients started to argue with me on that point.

"See, you're young, so you may not understand," I told

them. "Tyson was a brawler. His model was: Get in there, knock your opponent out in the first round. Ali was cocky, patient, sly and systematic. He was great at being confident. When his opponent had him up against the ropes, he'd make fun of him. What this did was two things. One, it worried his opponent, because he's hitting Ali with his best and strongest shots, but Ali's still poking fun at him! So, this has Ali's enemy thinking this guy is either crazy or invincible," I told the group. "And two. It helped Ali not to focus on the pain he was being dealt, but to tire out his opponent. Ali would start bobbing and weaving, shuffling his feet and dancing. Float like a *butterfly...*" I shouted and waited with my finger pointed to everyone.

They answered in unison, "Sting like a bee!"

"That's right. So when the drug, the bottle, the enemy or life in general has you against the ropes; when you're losing the fine fight of faith, *you gotta dance! You gotta dance! You gotta dance!* Let me hear you say it!"

"*You gotta dance!*" they hollered.

"You gotta what?"

"*You gotta dance!*"

The room rumbled with energy. Feeling like the coach of a football team rallying his players before the big game, I stood up and climbed onto my chair. "*You gotta what?*" They were fired up and rose to their feet. "*You gotta dance!*"

This was another pivotal moment in my life. Ever since then I've been thanking God for every day I was able to share my life's experiences with others and to help them.

* * *

My daughter was now four years old. I hadn't yet seen her, and I still didn't know her name. After countless attempts to see her and numerous restraining orders, Terry had decided to move out of state in 1994, without my knowledge. Thankfully, a short while later, I found out through a mutual friend that she and my daughter were back in town. That friend gave me Terry's address and I was determined to see my little girl.

I arrived at the front gate, nervous as hell, not knowing what to say, and holding a bouquet of flowers. I took a deep breath then stepped to the front door. Finally, I rang the bell.

A pretty, tall and lean five-year-old girl answered the door. That was my daughter. I was awestruck. My eyes immediately teared up. I crouched down on my heels and handed her the flowers. "Hello, how are you?"

"I'm fine," she replied with the most beautiful smile.

"Madison, who're you talking to?" Terry shouted somewhere from behind.

"Some man. He gave me flowers."

Terry bolted to the door. She pushed Madison out of the way and snatched the flowers out of her hands. "Go watch television, baby."

"But, Mommy—"

"Go watch television!"

Madison nonchalantly skipped off.

"How did you find me and what the hell are you doing here?"

"Madison, that's a lovely name."

"Michael, what the hell are you doing here?"

"I thought about her for five years nonstop. I want—no, I need to see my daughter."

"*My* daughter. You were relieved of all your fatherly duties when you told me you didn't want a relationship. Now goodbye!"

It was clear she was never going to allow me to get to know

Madison, so I had to go to the source that made everything possible. "You're a Christian, right?"

She laughed and rolled her eyes, as if to say: *Save that lame peacemaker's line for someone else.* "Don't bring God into this. The fact is I don't want my daughter around you, period! I still have a restraining order against you. Now get off my property or I'm calling the police," and slammed the door.

I didn't move. I wasn't gonna move. No, I was willing to be hauled off to prison if it meant getting a chance to hold my little girl for a moment. I stood at the door.

"Continue to love your enemies and to do good and to lend, not hoping for anything back," I recited to myself, "and your reward will be sons of the most high, because he is kind toward the unthankful and wicked. Continue to become merciful, just as your father is merciful. Stop judging and you will by no means be condemned. Keep on releasing, and you will be released."

With those words I turned and began walking away.

But the front door cracked open unexpectedly. Terry peered through the gap to say, "Wait." She took the latch off the door and opened it all the way. She didn't look too thrilled letting me inside her house, but I guess all those years of bitterness had eroded a bit, at last.

I stood at the door, stunned. Just inside, Madison sat on the floor playing with her dolls. I couldn't hold back the tears. "Well, your daughter's waiting for you. Would you come in so I can close my door? You're letting bugs in."

Hesitantly, like a kid on his very first day at school, I entered the house. I hugged my daughter and rubbed my fingers through her head. Then I listened to her say her ABC and count to a hundred. It was one of the greatest moments of my life. Unfortunately, it wouldn't last. For a few months, Terry allowed me to get to know Madison. Then, she met a man to whom she quickly got engaged, so she decided it was best I wasn't part of Madison's life. She got married in late 1996 and again relocated without my knowledge.

The sleepless nights, wondering how my daughter was doing, were hard to take. I determined that for my own sanity it would be better to let go and to keep it in God's hands. So far I had stood on the ropes of life and fought two near-death experiences, drugs, prison, disability, school, court, restraining orders and heartbreak. Some of those struggles were successful, with the help of God. The rest—well, I was now up against my next opponent. After waiting and arguing with my lawyers for five years about the lawsuit I had filed in 1991 against Brick-By-Brick, Inc., I received a letter from the courts informing me that my case was going to trial, at long last.

Obtaining that letter felt like the bricks had been lifted off of my shoulders—I felt it physically, mentally and spiritually, because I still harbored animosity over the accident. In fact, it was affecting me as a Christian. When the lawsuit was first issued, OSHA filed a number of reports with the company. However, the co-workers who witnessed the accident lied: they stated that I kept working even though we were told to stop, that I wanted to hurry up so we could go home for the night. So, going to trial was my opportunity to forgive. I had made up my mind that, no matter what was offered me out of court, I had to win or lose in a court of law. This wasn't a battle over money but over my soul.

* * *

The second floor office of Birkmen and Walls law firm was gargantuan, but it had a consistent, well-heeled style to it, down to the smells-like-money leather executive chairs and sofas. Not far from where I sat on one sofa were two polished, lemon-scented oak desks belonging to Kevin Birkmen and Susan Walls. Brick-By-Brick had made us a final offer of $200,000, and from either flanks my lawyers were trying to convince me to settle.

"Michael, the defendants are gonna use the fact that you shot a young white man and they're not going to let the court forget it. And if that's not enough, we're dealing with a ninety-eight percent white jury here. We'll never win!" Birkmen drilled.

"I trust that the jury is honest, hardworking people and... they're not gonna look at color," I answered.

"Look, they offered us two hundred thou—that's a lot of money."

I stood up and walked over to the gigantic picturesque window to look down on the city streets below. People moved about in silence, looking hopeless and worried. I couldn't relate to it, because I felt free and invincible.

"It's not about money," I said. "It's about justice. And I know that the jury will see that. Besides, my life is priceless. No amount of money will change what I had to suffer."

"Do you understand that there's a considerable chance we might lose, and then you'll get nothing. Take, the, money."

Kevin Birkmen—tall, slim and so persuasive he carried almost a sly demeanor—drew near me and placed his arm around my shoulder. Don't get me wrong; my lawyers were among the finest. But the hollow falsehoods he was about to peddle echoed inside my head before he even opened his mouth.

"Mike," he began, "I have a story for you. It's about a man standing on a mountain top. The floodwaters were rising and the man prayed to God to save him. Three times a boat came to his rescue and each time the man told the sailor that God will save him. Well, the man drowned. When he awoke he was in heaven. He went to St. Peter, and as he walked through the gates of heaven, he asked: 'Why didn't God save me?' St. Peter answered, 'God sent you three boats.' Mike, let us be your boat, let us save you."

"Let us save you from losing everything," Susan added.

I laughed, hysterically. When I turned my head to look out the window, my sight fell unexpectedly on the old wretched, drifting stranger, whom I hadn't seen since getting out of prison. He stared straight at me and held up another one of his cardboard signs. This time it read, IF YOU HAVE FAITH THE SIZE OF A MUSTARD SEED, YOU CAN MOVE MOUNTAINS (Matthew 17:20). God was again speaking directly to me.

I smiled and turned to my lawyers. "Counselors, get ready to move mountains and witness a miracle! I don't care how much money they offer. We're going to trial."

"I hope you know what you're doing," Susan said in exasperation.

"I don't, but God does."

I shook hands with them and was about to leave the office when Kevin made one last attempt to convert me. "Mike, think about what you're getting yourself..." I was already deaf to him and shut the door before he could finish his sentence. But a thought occurred to me.

I poked my head back into the office. "Why would a man entering heaven ask God why he didn't save him? He was in heaven, right? Eternally saved." I smiled and winked.

On June 17, 1996, we went to trial just as I said we would.

- 12 -

The trial was very long and stressful, lasting almost three months. At times I was just about ready to throw in the towel. On the last day of cross-examinations and closing arguments the courtroom was full. All the people I loved the most on this earth were here: Mac, Wayne, Ted, Tre, Eddie and my parents. Also in attendance were the big boys from the government agency, the OSHA environmental services. Something awesome was about to happen. I could feel it.

While my attorneys found this day the most nerve-racking of all, I sat cool and collected. I had been keeping a small pocket-sized bible with me throughout the trial, and knew I'd be fine no matter what the judgment would be. The lawyer for Brick-By-Brick Construction Inc., Robert Crocker, was cross-examining Ron McCormick, one of my co-workers who had witnessed the accident. "Could you tell court what you saw the day Mr. Daluz was injured?"

"The area that Mr. Daluz was working in was restricted. There was red tape blocking it off. Michael told me that he didn't care if it was deemed unsafe. He hoped...well, that something happened to him so he can sue the pants off of the company," Ron haltingly answered.

"Was everyone informed that the area was deemed restricted?"

"Yes."

Robert Crocker then glided over to the jury box like an elegant dancer. Wearing a smug smile on his face, he pursued, "So would you say that Mr. Daluz is trying to get a free ride off of Brick-By-Brick Construction?"

Ron guiltily glanced at me. "Oh, absolutely."

Kevin Birkmen slammed his fist on the counter and leaped out of his chair like a bug had just bit him. "I object!"

"Overruled," the judge decided.

"But, Your Honor, these statements are totally false."

"Sit down, Counselor."

The hot-blooded Birkmen took his seat and lividly scanned a pile of papers. I preserved my smile, and delicately patted him on the back. I simply refused to let these lies steal my joy.

"I have nothing further to say, Your Honor," Crocker stated.

"The witness may step down."

Ron left the stand doing his best to exit the courtroom as fast as he could. As he passed by, his head down, he browsed at me. I delivered him a merciful smile, because I truly wasn't angry with him. My purpose for the trial was to forgive.

During a thirty-minute recess, I strolled outside in the courthouse lobby. It was now down to the wire; the general anxiety over the coming ruling was palpable. I was drinking from the water fountain—my throat was so parched—when I spotted Ron exiting the building. I ran after him. "Ron!"

He turned around, looking a bundle of nerves. He appeared deeply ashamed, and started stammering. "Mike, I'm so sorry. I didn't want to do it, but they gave me a bonus and a raise. I'm going through a very bad financial—"

"I forgive you."

"What?"

"I just wanted to tell you that I forgive you. Take care of yourself, Ron."

Dumbfounded, he watched me cross the street.

I walked away feeling unstoppable. The weather was lovely, a cool 70 degrees. I ventured into a park and sat on a bench under a tall and wide tree. I'll never forget the utter serenity of this moment. An odd-looking but beautiful blue bird, a type I'd never before seen, flew over and landed on my knee. I stroked the bird's beak and something like a balm began to permeate my soul. I was looking at God's spirit come to comfort me.

I had to open my bible.

When I did, I fell on the most fitting passage: "It is reserved in the heavens for you, who are being safeguarded by God's power through faith for a salvation ready to be revealed in the last period of time. Indeed, you are greatly rejoicing, though for a little while at present it must be that you have been grieved by various trials in order that the tested quality of your faith be of much greater value than the gold that perishes, though it be proved by fire. Therein lies a reason for praise and glory and honor at the revelation of Jesus Christ. Though you never saw him, you love him. Though you are not looking upon him at present, you exercise faith in him and are greatly rejoicing with an unspeakable and glorified joy as you receive the end of your faith, the salvation of your soul."

I looked at my watch—2:15. It was time to head back to the courtroom. I closed the bible, and the bird took flight.

"Ladies and gentlemen of the jury, throughout this entire trial the defense has brought up my client's past criminal record. They said that he shot a young, hardworking and God-fearing all-American kid," Susan passionately declared, her high-heels echoing through the courtroom as she paced back and forth past the jury box. "Well, what about Michael? Prior to the 1987 incident, Mr. Daluz had no criminal record. The defendant also failed to mention that Michael is a U.S. Army vet, and he was a hardworking college student with a 3.6 GPA, when he was attacked and brutally beaten. But the bottom line, ladies and gentlemen, is that's not what we're here for today. We're here for justice. As in 1987, Mr. Daluz's life has been put in jeopardy by hateful individuals when the Brick-By-Brick, Incorporated, lied by saying the area known as Boiler 1 wasn't safe to work in, and that they ordered him to stop working but that Mr. Daluz refused. That makes no sense."

She was on the warpath. I watched Kevin Birkmen searching endlessly through papers in his briefcase.

Susan then turned to the folks in the audience and delivered an ironic depiction for effect: "Let's see, Michael was paralyzed on his right side for sixteen weeks. Over the last five and a half years he suffered from severe headaches, chronic back pain; he suffers from permanent double vision and PTSD. That really sounds like fun, like he's trying to get a free ride. Members of the jury, please—"

Out of the blue, Birkmen sprang to motion. Waving a document in the air, he interrupted Susan and leaped from his seat like he was on fire. "Your Honor, may I present the court with new evidence?"

"Objection, Your Honor!" Crocker cried out.

"Overruled. Counselor. You may approach the bench."

Birkmen stepped forward and handed the judge the sheet

of paper. The judge carefully examined it. Susan was as confused as I was. The judge handed the report to the bailiff, who in turn gave it to the jury, who passed it down the line for each juror to read.

"Ladies and gentlemen of the jury," Birkmen later explained, "I just found the original police report filed with OSHA and the New Haven Police Department, written by a former supervisor at Brick-By-Brick, Incorporated. It states that Michael Daluz was struck in the neck and the head while working in Boiler 1 after being told to continue working, even though it was deemed a high-risk area. And that if he didn't he would be fired. If you don't believe our side or the defendant, believe this single piece of paper. I have nothing more, Your Honor."

The judge turned to the men and women of the jury to inform them, "Members of the jury, it's been a long road and it's time to close this case. I need you to deliberate." The jurors stood up in unison and filed out of the jury box into a room. My stomach was in knots. This was the moment of truth.

Two hours later—the deliberation was relatively "swift"—I was on my knees praying and Birkmen and Susan were embracing me.

"In the case of Michael Daluz v. Brick-By-Brick, Inc., we the jury find the plaintiff zero percent at fault." The courtroom flew into a fracas.

Judge Daniels had to slam his hammer over and over for order, so I couldn't hear the foreman ending his declaration with: "The court awards Mr. Daluz $1.5 million in damages."

Neither did I hear nor did I care. I was only grateful to be free at last of all of the inconsequential feelings of being unloved which had haunted me since I was kid. I had come full circle to God's glory.

"That was very moving, Mr. Daluz," Judge Walker said to me. "You have been through a hell of a lot and you didn't give up. You're a true soldier and I admire that." "Still, in all, I'm not totally convinced, based upon your actions—kidnapping your daughter on the night of August 17, 2002—that you are able to take on the complete responsibility of being a single father."

"Your Honor, may I say one last thing?" I humbly requested.

"Sure."

"You're right, Your Honor. I may not be completely ready, but I will do anything for Bella. And yes, I agree, my actions were irresponsible and criminal. And I don't know how I will provide for my daughter. I'm in school full time and I work full time. But one thing I know for sure, that's God. He has brought me this far and he will deliver my daughter to me as well. God is love; therefore, I know love and that's what I will show my daughter everyday of her life."

Judge Walker rubbed his hands together, watchful for any discrepancies. It was then that my ex-wife became unruly. "Michael, you don't know God!" she screeched loudly.

"Mrs. Daluz, be quiet!"

"You'll never get my baby!"

"Bailiff, get her out of my courtroom."

The bailiff snatched Tracey by the arm and dragged her out kicking and screaming. "Michael, you ain't shit!"

It was amazing, because though I was back to square one—broke, divorced and going through a custody battle—I felt like Ali, the greatest.

- 13 -

"Daddy, can we go now?"

"Not yet, baby. Daddy has to dry the clothes," I told Bella. That was only a few months ago. Bella and I were in a Laundromat on a Saturday afternoon. While I studied two thick textbooks, she sat next to me brushing her baby doll's hair.

She's now six years old. She's bright, has a golden personality and she's beautiful. Although God's grand purpose for me is to help people, he was now training me for another championship fight: being a father. You see, I was awarded full custody of Bella in 2002. I will never give her up. We struggle, we go hungry sometimes, but together we'll make it. She's my world.

I am now 43 years old. It's been a twenty-year journey. A journey I'm still firmly embarked on, but I love it—both the good and the bad. I have earned my bachelor's and master's degrees as a drug rehabilitation clinician. I am currently studying for my Ph.D., only seven months away from becoming

"Dr. Daluz," a far cry from the ex-con and drug addict I used to be. At each stage of my studies, I have made the Dean's, the honor's and the presidential lists. Every morning I wake up at five to get ready for work. I wake Bella up, make her breakfast and then lunch, get her dressed and do her hair. Then we're out the door by 6:30. This is my life.

But that day at the Laundromat was unforgettable for another reason. It started out as any ordinary one. Then an old acquaintance walked in. At first I didn't recognize him. He was young, in his mid-thirties. He got busy repairing a machine but kept staring at me. Engrossed in study, so I paid no attention. Finally he approached me.

"Hey, long time no see. How are you?"

"I'm sorry, do I know you?"

"My name's Troy Gibson, and you're Michael Daluz. You were my counselor about ten years ago."

I put my books down and leaped off my seat. I couldn't believe my eyes. Troy looked healthy, had a muscular physic and a glow about him. "Oh, my God, little Troy?"

"Not so little anymore," he chuckled, patting his stomach. "I put on about forty pounds since you last saw me. That's what being clean will do for you."

"Well, you look great, kid."

"Thanks, I feel great! I've been clean for eight years now. My lady gave me a second chance and we're married with two children. I have my own maintenance company—contracts all over the tri-state area. And my wife and I just purchased our first home.

"That's awesome! God is good."

"Yes, he is. I guess believing isn't just a corny line from a Walt Disney movie after all. I prayed for the day when I'd see you again, so I can thank you and tell you that you inspired me. I owe it all to you."

"No, you don't. You owe it to God."

Troy drew and raised his fist toward me; I did mine. Our fists touched with a warmth of brotherhood no words could describe. With nothing left to say, Troy packed up his tools and bid me goodbye. I put my last load of clothes in the washing machine and sat back down to study some more.

That day left its imprint in my mind forever. Seeing Troy was another confirmation of God's miracles and power. And Bella was the icing on the cake. Sitting next to me, she reached inside her pocket and offered me three pennies.

"Daddy, here's some money to pay for the rent," she said. I smiled. She gave me a big hug and a kiss on the cheek. I picked her up and sat her on my knee. Facing the window, I spotted another friend outside—the old man.

He held a sign that said, I LEAVE YOU PEACE, I GIVE YOU PEACE. He smiled at me then wandered off into the sunset. I held Bella with all my might and looked up to the sun with tears of joy.

* * *

What I want to say is simple. With God all things are possible. When life has you against the ropes and you're losing the fine fight of faith, remember this: YOU GOTTA DANCE! YOU GOTTA DANCE! YOU GOTTA DANCE!

Made in the USA
Middletown, DE
04 September 2020

18260440R10073